THE MEMORIES WE KEEP

JENNIFER WALTERS

THE MEMORIES WE KEEP

Jennifer Walters

For my beautiful daughter, Alexis
Dream Big

The forty-five steps I climbed to enter the school depleted me of all my energy. It took everything I had not to turn around and walk back to my car. I wanted to go home and crawl back into my warm bed.

I pulled open the door, and let the little kids run past me. It was too late to turn back now. I nodded my head as the children said, "Good morning, Mrs. Jones."

I tried to smile, but my chest tightened as if hit by a line drive, and all I could do was nod at them. My lungs burned and were about as good as deflated balloons.

My heels clicked down the hallway, warning the teachers of my return. I put the weight on the balls of my feet to silence the echoing that bounced off the walls. Just a couple more steps to my classroom, and then I could breathe.

"Maddy." I heard the familiar voice call out from behind me.

I picked up my pace and let my heels hit the floor to block the sounds of her calling my name.

"Madeline, please wait," she said, louder.

I kept walking and looked straight ahead. I turned the

corner into my familiar old room and shut the door and locked it. I kept as quiet as possible, hoping she would walk right on past my room.

I was breathing hard, my back pushed tight against the door. I closed my eyes and listened for the sound of her shoes, her voice, her breathing.

A light knock, just knuckles tapping.

"Madeline, it's me, Whitney."

Silence. The tears ran down my face.

"I just wanted to say that I'm here if you need me. We don't have to talk about it. I can't imagine how hard it must be for you to come back here. I want you to know I'm here for you, okay? To talk, not to talk. Anyway, I'm here."

I thought she was gone, then she added, "Please don't shut me out. You're my best friend."

Silence.

"Okay, I can tell you need a few minutes so I'll go for now, but I'll be back later with my class."

Her footsteps echoed loud at first, then sounded farther and farther away. She was now in her room next door to mine.

I wiped the tears away with the back of my hand. I took a deep breath and walked around my library as if for the first time. It looked different, everything was different now. I was different. I wanted to hide behind the books in the dark and never be found.

Print-outs of Dr. Seuss with bright coloring hung all over the back wall with children's names written beneath each one. The one in the middle of the wall had a first-place ribbon taped to it. Dr. Seuss Week was one of my favorite weeks of the year, and I had completely forgotten. Tomorrow, March second, was his birthday. The calendar was on my desk with the themes of the days of Dr. Seuss week, and today just happened to be crazy hat day.

I pulled my tall red and white-striped hat out of the back cupboard and tied the bright red bow around my neck. Anything to distract me from my broken heart. No one could take me seriously or give me looks of pity when we were all dressed so goofy. This would be a good week.

Reality set in. Who was I kidding? This would be a terrible week.

The bell rang for the school day to start. Time to rip off the band-aid. Right there on the bookshelf was my favorite Dr. Seuss book. I hugged it tight to my chest with one hand and opened my classroom door with the other. My stomach tightened in sync with the turn of my wrist. Breathe, just breathe. The sound of my therapist's words echoed in my mind: *Day one is the hardest, but just put one foot in front of the other. It will get better with time.* It seemed impossible to me at that moment, but I had no choice. I had no one to take care of me now. I was all alone, forever.

THE FIRST CLASS came in around eight forty-five. I was running around, putting books back where they belonged and displaying the Dr. Seuss books on the top shelf because the kids had an easier time finding the books when they were smack dab at eye level.

That was the thing about subs, they had no idea how to be a librarian. I'd be finding books out of place all week, but it would be a great distraction. Organizing books soothed my soul better than anything else. I loved everything neat and in place. My therapist diagnosed me with OCD, obsessive compulsive disorder, but what was wrong with wanting everything a certain way?

Whitney led her class into the library and to the hand sanitizer station. I directed them onto the carpet. Although the pandemic was somewhat over, hygiene was never better

3

with the children. Not one of their faces was familiar to me, and I was embarrassed for ghosting my best friend just moments before. I tried not to make eye contact with Whitney. Maybe she would slip out and not say anything to me about earlier. I was grateful five-year-olds could not sense the tension in the room.

A little girl came up and tugged on my skirt. "Teacher, where is Mrs. Anderson?"

Whitney hurried over to the child and redirected her by pointing at the empty spot on the alphabet carpet.

"Ladies and gentlemen, hands on your heads, please." Only about half of them followed her direction. "Hands on your heads," she repeated in a higher decibel. The whole class followed in silence.

"Now in your lap." All eyes were on her, including mine. "Remember how Mrs. Anderson was filling in for Mrs. Jones? Well, this is Mrs. Jones, and she is our real librarian."

Some kids shook their heads and some nodded.

Whitney nervously adjusted her elephant hat. She'd worn that hat since we started teaching ten years ago. We were strangers back then, practically kids ourselves when we started working here. I was from Side Lake, a lake town twenty or so miles away. She was from The Twin Cities area in southern Minnesota, which stood for the big cities of Minneapolis/St. Paul.

We soon found out her husband and I graduated from high school together in Hibbing, so we had a lot to talk about and instantly became friends. She shared my passion for reading, and we both got pregnant around the same time. Her Brittany and my Ariel started kindergarten together last year, and we even took them school clothes shopping together. Whitney and her husband bought a house on McCarthy Beach Road in Side Lake, and I lived just off Turtle Creek Road on West Sturgeon, not too far from them. West Sturgeon was a part of the chain of five lakes.

As soon as I had Ariel and came back from maternity leave, Whitney was going on maternity leave. After she had Brittany, she watched Ariel so I did not have to worry about daycare. We were like sisters since neither of us had any siblings. We did everything together, and we were even known to finish each other's sentences. But now just looking at her made my heart ache.

Whitney kept talking to her students. "Well, Mrs. Jones is a very fun teacher and look at her hat. It's truly the hat from *The Cat and the Hat*."

All the kids giggled.

"Can I wear your hat?" The little girl with the Cindy Lou Who braids said.

"We already talked about this when Jacob stole Tommy's hat this morning kids, remember? We keep our hands to ourselves and our hats on our heads or we lose them. Now let's give our full attention to my friend and our librarian, Mrs. Jones." She did a little silent clap and the kids followed her lead.

"Thank you, Mrs. Thomas. Does everyone know what week this is?"

"Dr. Seuss week," they all said in unison.

"You are all correct, great listening ears. Is that why I'm wearing this silly hat?"

They responded with giggles, like they did every year.

"How many of you have read this book?" I held up the book for all of the class to see.

A few hands raised and one little boy stood up on his knees, blocking the kids' view from behind him.

"Sit down, please. I can't read until everyone sits on their bottoms."

By the time I finished reading *Wacky Wednesday*, their

attention span was gone. "Boys and girls, you may now find the book you want to check out and make sure to bring it to me at my desk so I can scan it. Then you can sit down at your table spot and read quietly, okay?"

I was not used to kindergartners walking, not running. They knew exactly where to go and what to do the first time I had them in my library and gave them directions to follow. I did not miss the craziness of September this year when they had no idea what they were doing and classes were a chaotic mess. It did hurt to know someone else helped teach them, someone else guided them in the right direction while my whole world fell apart. The school did not stop for me. It kept going like nothing had happened.

I heard a knock on my door and the principal walked in. I had to look away. Why was he here? He said hello to the children and walked toward me. The kids were asking him questions, and I contemplated jumping out the window. That would be the only way to make this conversation easier.

"I need to speak with Mrs. Jones for one-minute, okay, kids? Now I need you all to be on your best behavior."

He took off his Vikings hat and stepped closer to me. It took everything I had not to take a step back. I looked down at my feet. That was the best I could do.

"How are you doing? I'm sure the first day back isn't easy for you, but I promise I will do everything I can to make sure this isn't weird."

"Why would it be weird?"

He let out a loud exhale. He glanced away, toward the children waiting in line at my desk, then he looked back at me. "You know what I mean. It's going to take some time, but I think we can get through this."

"Principal Jones, nothing about this is normal. You coming to talk to me about this isn't even a tiny bit normal.

6

We are supposed to be in a professional setting. No personal issues. That was your rule, remember?"

He leaned in and whispered, "You're right, Madeline. I'm sorry. I guess I just--"

"Everyone, say goodbye to Principal Jones." I interrupted him loudly to make sure all the kids heard me. My words should get him to leave. I hoped.

Some kids waved, but most were so lost in side conversations or their noses were deep in their books that they had no idea I was even speaking to them. If I hadn't been so angry with him for trying to talk to me, the kids' focus on reading would have impressed me.

He looked into my eyes, then back at the kids. "Goodbye, kids. Have a great day." He walked out the door, and I started breathing again.

How dare he come in during class and act like he cared about how I was doing. He hadn't even talked to me in months. I sat down at my desk and did what any librarian would do. I checked out books for the kids with a smile, then started a Dr. Seuss cartoon on the projector.

The rest of the morning went much better. The principal stayed out of the library, and at lunch I ate in my room all by myself. I shut and locked the door because I did not want any visitors. I needed to make it through the day.

My last class of the day would be the hardest because Lisa Banks was my least favorite teacher and person on the planet. She came in with her nose in the air and her hands behind her back as she led her second-grade class in and onto the rug.

SECOND-GRADERS WERE much different than kindergartners. Not just a height difference, but in listening and self-control. The children sat down with their hands in their laps. They signaled their teacher that they had zipped their lips with an imaginary zipper .

"Class, you all remember Miss Jones, don't you?"

The reference was more than a surprise.

Justin, the little boy in the front row wearing glasses raised his hand.

I pointed at him. "Hello Justin. Do you have a question?"

"I'm glad you're back, Mrs. Jones."

I smiled.

"Miss Jones," Lisa said.

I wanted to tell her to get lost. But that would be frowned upon in my position and it would not set a good example for the children.

"Thank you, Justin," I said, not even looking in Lisa's direction.

"Why were you gone? Because your daughter died?" Justin said.

I was not expecting that from him. I knew it would probably come up, and I needed to face it, but I did not want to explain what happened in front of Lisa, of all people.

"You aren't supposed to say that, you dummy," little Heather Bliss said. She hit her forehead with her palm.

I always liked that girl.

"Don't mind him. I'm sorry about what happened to Ariel, Miss Jones," Heather said.

Lisa finally stepped forward. "Okay kids. Let's be quiet now, and let Miss Jones speak. This isn't the time to ask these types of questions. I'm sure she does not want to talk about it."

Her words had no emotion in them. She did not have a bit of empathy for my little girl, not one bit.

"It's okay to talk about Ariel, but right now we are going to talk about the great writer, Dr. Seuss. Did you know he wasn't actually a doctor? Tell me why they called him Dr. Seuss, then."

"Wasn't it because his dad always wanted him to be a doctor and practice medicine?"

"That is correct, Heather. His father always wanted him to practice medicine, but he wasn't actually a doctor of anything. An honorary doctorate was granted to him by Dartmouth in 1956."

Johnny sat up a little taller. "What's Dartmouth?".

"Dartmouth is the name of a college. He could use the title Dr. Seuss because it was his pen name. Does anyone know what a pen name is?"

Lisa finally left my classroom. What a day. I needed to chat with Whitney after school about what Lisa was telling her class. I had been avoiding her all day, afraid I would get emotional, but she was my best friend. It wasn't possible to avoid her forever, and I hadn't returned her calls or answered the door since my life went to hell. But I was back at school teaching, and for the first time in months, I did not think about Ariel every second of the day. Maybe once every minute, which was a huge progress.

THE SECRETARY WAS NOT at her desk when I walked into the office to get my mail. She was another person I'd been avoiding my first day back. She never liked me. She was always rude and tried to tell the teachers what to do all the time. Some actually listened because they were scared of her. Lisa Banks was friends with her, likely because it made her nastiness more powerful to have the evil secretary on her side. Lisa picked and chose which staff she liked, and I did not make the cut. I can't say it hurt my feelings at all.

I pulled out my pile of mail. The school had purchased a new paper cutter. It looked like a large Cricut. I went to check it out and heard voices in the office. I stepped behind the wall. One of the voices was Principal Brad Jones, my ex-husband and the father of my child.

Brad's voice carried. I always told him I could hear him before I could see him. Now he was my boss, but no longer the man I would be spending the rest of my life with. Seeing him and talking to him after all these months was not easy. It hurt.

"Hey, Brad. I bought some steaks with plans to pull out my grill and have my first barbecue of the year since it's finally above fifty degrees. Would you like to come over and have dinner with me?" a women's voice said.

My stomach was flip-flopping at the thought of Brad with another woman. We had a child together. Ariel hadn't even been gone for a year, and here he was planning a date with one of the teachers.

Sure, I was disconnected from my old life at the school and all the teachers who were once my friends. They tried to stop by after the accident, but even when I knew they could see me through the sliding glass door, I could not bring myself to answer the door. I did not want to talk to anyone. I would curl up on the couch in front of the television binging Netflix or run inside when I saw their cars pull up. No one understood my behavior was not personal. I did not want to talk to anyone. Still, who would ask out my ex-husband my very first day back at work? I was pretty sure I knew the answer.

I knew what I had to do. I could not bear to hear his answer, so I walked out of the mailroom right past them, but it was too late.

"That is very thoughtful of you," Brad said. "But I told you before I'm not ready. I just got a divorce--"

I looked right at Lisa, her mouth wide open in shock,

mirroring Brad. She was probably embarrassed I heard her get turned down.

"Hello." I looked into her eyes, smiled, and then glared just a step away from her.

She stared blankly and although my chest was heavy and I could hardly breathe, I was so glad I witnessed him turn her down. Not that I cared who he dated. His life was no longer any of my business, and it was only a matter of time before he would no longer be able to use the divorce as an excuse.

2

I had good intentions of visiting Whitney in her classroom to make amends, but I would fall apart when I told her what I heard, and I didn't have it in me to apologize for right now. I wanted to put Brad in the back of my mind, not think about him until therapy after school.

MY THERAPIST'S office was right on the main road in the middle of town. I'd been meeting with him for almost six months now, and I still cried throughout every visit. At first I was a bit apprehensive on whether or not I actually wanted to see a shrink, but I stopped talking to pretty much everyone I knew so this was my only social time.

I liked that he was calm, and that he let me vent and really listened and handed my tissues as if on cue. At this point he would just hand the tissues to me when I walked in the door. In no way did I take it as an insult. The gesture automatically made me smile every time.

I sat down in the comfy blue chair and pulled out a tissue from the box and then placed the box next to me on the table. I looked around at the two walls that held books. The sight of them calmed me as I was always nervous at the start of our appointments.

"Today was your first day back at work, wasn't it?"

I nodded.

He crossed his legs and seemed to be waiting for my answer, but instead I fidgeted with the tissue in my hand, nervous to look up.

"Well, how did it go?"

I looked back at the wall of books behind him when I spoke. "Not well."

"Tell me about it."

"Well, my anxiety was on high alert, and the only time I felt okay was when I was in my room surrounded by books. I took deep breaths, and I made it through the day, but Brad kept trying to get me to talk. It was terrible."

"I'm sure there are still some strong feelings for both of you."

I did not have feelings for Brad, that was long over. "Not me."

"Now, Madeline, both of you decided your marriage was over, but you will forever be connected. He was the love of your life, but the truth is the two of you went through a very traumatic event. Some people make it through stronger after the loss of a child, but some can't come back from that kind of grief and trauma together. There is no right or wrong way." He pushed his glasses up the bridge of his nose. "Have you thought about asking him for more details about what happened that day?

I shook my head. "No way. It was an accident, and she's gone. I don't want to think about how horrible it was, and I don't want Brad to relive it. That is just horrible."

"Have you ever considered he may want to talk about it, share it with you?"

"Why would he want to?"

"It might give you both some closure."

"I don't want closure. I want my daughter back."

Like he had any idea what it felt like to lose a child. Did he think I was going to forget her? That I wanted to know the vivid details? Nothing was going to bring her back. No one should ever have to feel this kind of pain. We are supposed to die before our children. This was not fair or right. Why Ariel?

Losing Ariel felt like my heart was ripped out of my chest and stomped on over and over until I was numb. Here I was, stuck alone on this horrible planet knowing my daughter was no longer with me. She did not have the opportunity to look up at the same sun or moon as I did. Never again would I snuggle with her or read her a bedtime story. She would never graduate from high school or get married and have a family of her own.

"Did you get to speak with Whitney like you wanted?"

"No, because stupid Lisa Banks, teacher I was telling you about who has a crush on Brad asked him out on my first day back at the school, and I heard her do it."

He wrote something down in his notebook. I searched his face for some kind of reaction, but he didn't seem to have one. How do therapists keep such poker faces? Was there some kind of class they had to get down that unemotional stare?

"And how did that make you feel?"

"Angry as hell."

"Why?"

"Why? Why?" As I repeated his question out loud, I was unsure of the answer.

"Yes. You wanted the divorce, correct?"

I crossed my arms in front of me to stop my fidgeting. "Well, yeah. I don't want to be with him if that is what you're asking. Brad knows about my past with Lisa. I just don't ever want him to be with her."

"What do you want?"

"Not that."

"Do you know what I think?"

My eyes burned, and I was one emotional feeling away from crying. The thought of Brad and Lisa together made my stomach turn.

I told him about the rest of my day and my plan to finally talk to Whitney tomorrow. As I got up to leave, he surprised me.

"I think today was a lot more progressive with your grieving than you think."

I wiped my wet eyes with what was left of the tissue after sobbing throughout our appointment. "Why is that?"

"You may be angry, but you're finally feeling again."

"I cry every time I'm here. I have been feeling."

"This is something other than grief. It's a step in the right direction. You are thinking outside of just your family again."

"I think you are the crazy one to think my husband getting hit on is a good thing. Maybe I need a new therapist because you seem to be losing it."

He opened the door for me and laughed. "See you next week?"

"As long as you have a box of tissues ready."

SOME NIGHTS I had nightmares about her. I was chasing her, but I could never catch her. I heard her crying and screaming for me, reaching her sweet little arms out for me, but I could not get to her. Other nights I didn't sleep at all. Maybe my therapist was right when he told me I was worried if I went to sleep the nightmares would return.

The day of her death loomed over me. I was too busy

planning her birthday party to be cautious. I wanted to have everything perfect so I let her go to the Children's museum without me. I needed her out of the house so she wasn't in the way of my decorating. Everything just had to be perfect. What was wrong with me? I forgot what was important, her safety, and now she was gone.

I kept her bedroom door shut, and I very seldom opened it. But some nights I would go into her room and sleep in her bed, smelling her sweet baby shampoo still lingering on her pillow. But most of the time I was too afraid to go into her room. I wanted it to be just the way she left it.

Now I was all alone in my dream house on the lake. I always thought living on the lake would take away all my troubles, but living there without my family took away the joy. The view was breathtaking, but what was a house that was no longer a home? My family was gone, and I was alone.

I sat down on the deck that looked over the water. The temp was still a little chilly, and we were bound to have a couple more snowstorms before spring when the lake opened up. Living in Minnesota, we expected the unexpected because the weather was nowhere near consistent. It could be seventy degrees one day and the next day below zero or a snowstorm was coming. The weather was a lot like my life these days.

My therapist warned me not to make any big changes in the first year after the two big losses in my life. In two months it would be one year, and then I would change everything. I was ready to leave the school and possibly do nothing for a while. Maybe sell this house and move down south where no one knew my past and the sun shined every day. I could not see my now ex-husband every day at work, I just couldn't. When I looked at him, I felt angry and bitter. I wanted Ariel back. It wasn't fair she was gone forever.

. . .

DAY TWO ARRIVED and hopefully was not a repeat of yesterday.

I heard the footsteps behind me, but I could not get myself to turn around.

"Maddy, Maddy, can I have a minute?"

Brad. I opened my door and closed it, locking it behind me. The doorknob turned and then a knock.

"Maddy, I know you can hear me. I really need to speak with you."

I heard the sadness in his voice, but I could not face him. "I don't want to talk to you. Don't you think you've done enough? Just leave me alone."

"Maddy."

I jumped at the voice behind me. Whitney was sitting at the little kid's table in my room. I was half crying, half laughing as I held my chest with my open hand. "Whitney, what are you doing here?"

She got up and walked to my side. She pulled me in tight for a hug and would not let me go.

I fought her at first, but then like magic, all the tension left my body, and the tears started. Why had I been hiding from her? I remembered why she was my best friend. This was why. She was always there for me, and even when I pretty much ghosted her, here she was with open arms.

"You dealt with your first day back at school without even looking at me. I hate to see you like this. Let it out," she said. "It's okay, it's just you and me."

"I don't know how to stop the pain. I'm so sorry," I said, sobbing into her shoulder. "I'm just so numb."

"Don't be sorry. I'm sorry."

I pulled away. "For what?"

"For not trying harder. If I was a better friend, I would have kept calling and showing up at your door. I failed you."

I laughed through my sobs. I could no longer see her

through the blurriness of my tears. "I'm so sorry I haven't called you back. If it makes you feel any better, I haven't talked to anyone in weeks. You didn't fail me. I made it pretty impossible for you."

I was pretty sure my mom called her multiple times out of concern because I stopped calling my mom back, too. I even went as far as to change my locks so the key my mom had would no longer work. "Can I ask you something?"

She nodded. "Of course. Anything."

"How long has Lisa been coming on to him?"

She crossed her arms and looked away, her face a light shade of red. "Why, what happened?"

"I was around the corner in the mailroom, and I heard her ask him on a date. She didn't know I was there so it wasn't just to be evil."

"Still. Listen, she wishes Brad was into her, but he's not. It's obvious he only has eyes for you. You know how she is."

"Not anymore. We got divorced for a reason."

"He will always love you. He's not ready for a relationship, especially not with her."

"How long has she been doing this?"

"She's been there for him, supporting him, and cooking him food since the two of you split, but he keeps telling her she's a great friend."

I could finally breathe. I needed to sit down. Brad would not give in and go out with the one person I hated most in this world, would he? He knew our history, the way she treated me. He wouldn't do that to me.

"Don't let her get to you. You know she's always been jealous of you and Brad."

Whitney knew every detail of my history with Lisa. She knew we were best friends growing up, and she knew there was a lot of friction between us after our falling out. We grew apart, and she started hating me but never told me why.

I was sure it was because she had a crush on Brad, and she thought I was getting in the way of the relationship she wanted with him. She did not understand he was just never into her that way. It was easier for her to blame me instead.

"Why don't you and I go to Boomtown tonight and have avocado burgers and cheese curds."

"I don't know."

"Oh, come on, you know you love their cheese curds and their peanut butter beer," she said with a toothy smile.

She just had to dangle that above my head. She knew I never said no to Boomtown.

"Oh, I don't know." I groaned, and I'm pretty sure my stomach growled at the thought. "It's really hard for me to say no. Do you know how long it's been since I went out? I had a hard enough time just getting dressed this morning."

"A night out will be good for you, and get your mom off your back. Plus, you're looking so thin. I'm worried about you."

"You don't need to be."

Was it that obvious I hardly ate? I didn't have the appetite I used to. I was in no way starving myself, but I did have to make myself eat.

She gave me another hug and opened the door. I stiffened. Was Brad still out there, waiting to sneak in? I looked down the hall, but he was gone.

I returned to the library, my classroom for the past ten years. All the memories over the years flooded in. The 'before the accident' moments and memories.

I could almost see Ariel curled up on a bean bag in the back corner like it was yesterday. The day I was making out with Brad in the back closet, and Whitney busted us. Back before Ariel was born, we could not keep our hands off each other. Throughout our marriage, I could never open a door when he was around. He would swoop in and open it before

I had a chance. He took pleasure in treating me like a princess, from foot massages to cooking dinner after a long day of work. I would joke that if anything happened to him, I would not know how to pump my own gas. He would laugh. "I'm not going anywhere," he'd say. Well, he was wrong. I never imagined something like this would happen. Every mother's biggest fear.

This room was so much more than a children's library. Being surrounded by books helped to calm my nerves, and it felt good to have something to look forward to. But in the back of my mind, I felt as though I shouldn't be having fun when my baby girl was no longer in this world. Where was she? Was she all alone? Was I even considered a mother anymore? This world no longer made any sense to me.

I COULD NOT GET to my car fast enough after school. I made my way out the door and that's when I saw Brad standing next to his truck, which happened to be parked next to my car. He was on the phone, but luckily staring off to the road, his back to me. I snuck around the building and down the street.

As I rounded the corner and the hospital came into view, I stopped in my tracks. I saw the woods and followed the hidden trail to the pond and the bridge. The woods were dreary and dark. The winter snow and bitter cold had killed all of nature like a death blanket squeezing all the color out. Much like what I imagined my heart looked like. I stepped around clumps of snow on the path with my short heels.

I remembered how many days I spent there after Ariel died. The scenery calmed me. It was my solace when I wanted to be alone to remember her.

I sat on the bench in the middle of the woods that was ironically in the middle of town. I thought back all too clearly to the beauty of this area in the summer when everything was in bloom and the trees and grass were so green. Minnesota green.

I now referred to everything as before the accident or after the accident. My life changed forever in just a moment of time. I missed her so much.

The trees were bare, not a squirrel, bird, or duck in sight. Funny how in just a few weeks the trees would be budding and blooming again, and the animals would come out of hiding. The birds would sing in the trees and fly through the sky.

The water in the pond had a layer of ice covering the top. Not enough to hold the weight of a human without cracking and breaking.

I set my bag down on the ground. A voice behind startled me.

"Maddy?"

I turned.

"I thought I'd find you here. Maddy, aren't you cold? You should have a jacket."

I had so many things I wanted to say to him, but the anger in my veins took over. I stared at him. "What the hell, Brad? Why can't you just leave me alone? Didn't you do enough already?"

"I had to talk to you, but you just keep running. You aren't alone, you know. I hate the way everything turned out. I never wanted this. Any of this."

I turned around and stared toward the pond. "It's not a competition, and it looks like you are moving on just fine."

That really wasn't fair, but I could not stop myself. I was so angry.

Sticks crunched beneath his feet until he was standing next to me. The wind blew the familiar scent of him toward me. I closed my eyes, the aroma taking me back to all those wonderful years we spent together falling in love. Back then we would have made out right here in the woods. I opened my eyes. Those times were over long ago. There was no *us* anymore.

I folded my arms and turned to see his face. "Why did you follow me here?"

He stared at the ground, his hands in his pockets. He looked so vulnerable, so different from the strong, tough personality everyone saw in school.

"Well?"

"I know the past year hasn't been easy, but I think we need to call a truce."

"A truce? Really?" I picked up my bag and put it over my shoulder. "Don't worry, I will be more professional at work, boss. Have a good day."

"Please, don't be like that," he said.

I just turned and walked away.

I was rude and out of line, but to say I hated him was an understatement. I had been at the school ten years, and he had been there a little longer than that. He was finally the principal and we were, well ... nothing anymore. Couldn't he understand I needed some space and fewer reminders of him?

I made it back to my car without any sign of Brad following me. Was he still at the pond? Was he thinking about Ariel? Of our life together all those years? Did he care, or was he just trying to make it less awkward at work? I hated the thought of him and Lisa ever being together. Would he give in and go out with her? The thought stung.

I FORGOT how beautiful Boomtown was. The high ceilings, the open room with new hardwood floors, and the antique brick walls in the atrium side showed how historic the building was. A brewery hid in the basement, but the beer vats were visible and secured straight ahead of me in a glass viewing for show.

The restaurant was originally named Zimmy's after the famous singer, Bob Dylan (Bob Zimmerman). The town was proud of his success, and tourists visited his childhood home. Even the street he grew up on had a sign with the words Bob Dylan Drive in front of his childhood home and a crosswalk with music bars and music notes painted in the street out front. Zimmy's was sold years ago and remodeled. The place looked even more beautiful than it had before.

I asked for a table in back so I could hide from anyone I might know. I did not want to make small talk with anyone but my best friend.

Our home-brewed peanut butter beer arrived in big glasses, and I took my first sip. The simple act of drinking a beer gave me a sense of a little bit of normal coming back into my life.

I wanted to steer the conversation away from me for as long as possible. "So how are you? It's been a long time, and I want to hear what's new with you."

"Okay, well Josh and I are going to Florida on vacation at the end of the year, and Brittany ..." She stopped and turned bright red.

"Whit, don't stop talking about your daughter for my sake. I love Brittany. Just because she was best friends with Ariel doesn't mean I don't want to hear about her anymore. Now tell me, I'm your best friend. I want to know all about what I've missed."

"I know you're hurting, and I don't want to hurt you anymore or lose you again. Ariel was like another daughter to me, and it hurt when I lost the both of you."

I pushed down the anger. She was trying to tell me the

way she felt, but she did not know what it was like. She still had Brittany. I took a long, hard gulp of my beer.

"Brittany what now?"

"Um, well, we put her in basketball, and it has been quite an experience. Let's just say she does more cartwheels than anything. We thought it would be a good idea after ... you know, everything she's been going through."

I struggled to find the right words. "I'm sure it hasn't been easy for her. Losing her best friend."

"No, I really don't think she understands completely. I'm sorry, I probably shouldn't have said anything, and I'm even more sorry that I keep saying sorry."

And this is why I'd been hiding from the world. When I lost my daughter, everyone around me was so worried about what they should and shouldn't say, they had no idea how to act normal when they were around me. I craved normal. I did not want anyone to forget about Ariel, but they acted like I would fall apart any minute if they mentioned her name. Like I what, forgot she died?

"It's okay, Whit. I'm glad you told me, and I think it's a great idea to keep her busy. I'm sure it isn't easy for her either."

"We just miss her so much."

I placed my hand on hers. "I know you're still a mom, and I'm sorry I've been so distant, but I'm still me and I'm still your best friend so don't filter everything around me. Yes, it's difficult to hear, but I need that. Sometimes I forget I wasn't the only one who lost her, you know. It affected everyone who knew her."

"True, but you're her mom," she said. "It's the hardest for you. Just remember, I'm here, always. Please don't shut me out again, okay?"

I smiled and nodded. "Can I ask you a question?"

Whitney shifted her weight and crossed her legs nervously. "Of course."

I took a drink, unsure of whether I really wanted to know the answer. "Do you think Brad is responsible for what happened to Ariel?"

She cleared her throat. "I'm not really sure. I don't know exactly what happened. All I can say is he would have given his life for her, if he had the chance. As would you."

She was right, but I never really talked to him about the specifics that night. He tried, but I told him I did not want to hear it. She was gone and nothing would change that.

"Brad has changed a lot since the accident and you know ... the divorce, if you haven't noticed."

"What do you mean, changed?"

"He's cold and distant. He walks around in a daze, always so angry. He used to be, well, approachable. I'm not saying it's anyone's fault. I think he's just really hurting. I think he feels guilty for what happened."

Sometimes I felt so alone, like I was the only one who lost a child. He was not the best when it came to showing his feelings. I was unsure of how he was holding himself together.

"How is everything between the two of you since you've been back at the school? I saw him trying to chase you down this morning. That can't be easy."

"After everything happened, we fought a lot about the accident. He tried so hard to talk to me about what happened. He did not understand that I didn't want to hear the awful details. I knew they were hit driving to Grand Rapids when she was killed. It was an accident and no one was drinking. Why would I want to know every detail? I'd never be able to get it out of my head. I feel like he's trying to get me alone to discuss it. I'm just not ready yet."

"Well, maybe one day you will be ready to hear it, and

then you can ask him. Who knows, it might give you some ... closure." Her cheeks turned rosy. "Closure to what happened, I mean. Answer some of your questions."

"I know what you mean, but I'm not ready yet. I don't want to know every detail, you know? I feel sick at even the thought."

"I can't imagine. I think he's just having a hard time keeping all of that in. Not being able to talk to you about it."

"I guess. Has he been that moody at school?"

"He blows up pretty easy. I just worry one of these days he really loses it and risks his job. He's not focused anymore."

I nodded, but I could not imagine him being as angry at school as Whitney led on. She had to be mistaken. Maybe she was assuming too much. What was I supposed to do about it anyway? We never even talked anymore.

"Do you still have feelings for him? I know the two of you have been through a lot, but you were so great together."

"No, I don't want to be with him. It's so awkward already. The last time I worked at the school he was the assistant principal and we were together. Now it's as though he's on a mission to have this talk with me every time he sees me, and Lisa gets under my skin. What is her problem anyway?"

Whitney tried to get our waitress's attention and pointed to our drinks. "Maddy, don't let her get to you. That's what she wants. She's evil, and she's always had a crush him."

"I've lost everything. I wish she would leave me alone. Leave Brad alone."

Whitney snapped her fingers. "I know you're hurting, but I won't let you be depressed, not anymore. You're an upbeat person, and you and I both know Ariel wouldn't want her mom to be this unhappy. She'd want you to live your life. Am I right?"

For the first time, I thought about Ariel's death in a different way. What she said made sense. I was angry and I removed myself from the world and all my friends. "I think you have a good point. But it's hard. This pain in my chest won't go away. It feels like an elephant is standing on top of me all the time and jumping on my lungs."

Whitney brought her hand to her chest. "I can't imagine." She leaned into the table. "I don't expect you to help Brad. He isn't your problem anymore. But I wanted you to know because he's your boss now, and I don't want you to take his moodiness to heart. I hope you don't have to see it. He still loves you. You must see it. The way he follows you around and tries to talk with you and make sure you are okay. I know he still loves you. It's good to see him having some emotions again. Even if it doesn't feel that way, it's quite an improvement for him."

"Well, I know I will never be happy, but life has to be better than this. I want to step out of my comfort zone and get out of my house, even if the idea seriously makes me ill. Do you have any ideas? You did get me to this restaurant, which I thought was impossible."

She grinned, and her eyes gleamed with mischief. "I have so many ideas, but I can't think of one right this second. I'm in shock, give me a minute."

"Take a day or two to think about it." What was I getting myself into? I knew my best friend better than anyone. I was not going to like what she came up with. Maybe that was exactly what I needed. By giving her the reigns, I did not have to climb out of this hole all by myself.

The next morning, Whitney pretty much skipped her way into the library, humming what sounded like *Mary Had a Little Lamb*.

I looked up from the stacked books in front of me. My sub obviously had no knowledge of how alphabetical order worked. I had piles of books out of place after going through just the first two aisles of shelves.

"Well, you're sure cheerful. I guess you had less to drink than me last night. I have one heck of a headache."

She sat down next to me with perfect posture and a big, toothy smile.

"Why do I have a feeling this is about you planning out my happiness?"

"Because it is."

She took the book out of my hand and set it down on the bookshelf. "Stop for just one minute. I need your full attention because my ideas are going to change your life."

"Okay. I asked for it. Proceed."

She ignored my sarcasm. "I will start leaving you notes in your mailbox with steps to take, instructions you need to follow that will lead you right to your happiness. Follow whatever steps I give you--to the best of your ability, okay?"

"I have a bad feeling about this. Remember, I will get you back if you go too crazy."

"I will be a good friend, I promise. You just have to trust me and promise me one thing."

I tried to rub away the headache at my temples. My head was pounding. Whether it was from the beer last night or my best friend's crazy ideas, I could not be sure. "What's that?"

"You'll follow my instructions no matter what."

I stared at her.

"Maddy, please. Do you trust me?"

"I have no choice," I said.

"Yay!"

I rested my head on my open hand after raising my eyebrows at her.

"Remember I have your best interests at heart. I would never do anything to hurt you. It will be good for you to get out of your comfort zone." She paused. "One more thing."

It was always one more thing with Whitney. I shot her a challenging look, which she ignored.

"You have to open the note right away and check your mailbox when you get to school and when you leave so you don't miss one. I don't want the note to be out of date by the time you read it."

"How long are we planning on doing this?"

"How about until school gets out?"

I was going to regret what I said next, but I needed a change in my life and maybe this was the way to achieve it. "Deal."

She jumped out of the chair and hugged me with way too much enthusiasm. "You're going to love this so much."

I was going to regret this so much.

.   .   .

THE NEXT MORNING I removed the pink envelope from my mailbox. My name was on the front in Whitney's handwriting. I grabbed the rest of my mail and waited until I was in the library before I opened it.

Dear Maddy,

There is nothing better than starting the day off with a good laugh. Tell one of your classes a kids' joke or two or three. That's it. (See I told you this was going to be easy!) Have a wonderful day. I can't wait to hear all about it :).

XO Whit

OKAY, so this one was not so bad. It was kind of silly, actually. Before Whitney and I had kids, we would go to amateur night in Minneapolis, stay the weekend, and I would tell jokes and she would read poetry. Sometimes my jokes would not go over well with the audience, but sometimes, when it all clicked, they laughed so hard. That did not happen often, but I had so much fun doing it. Putting myself out there was exhilarating. I knew no one there, and no one knew me so if they did not like me, no problem. I would probably never see them again. Those were days I long left behind me after marrying Brad and having Ariel. That was years ago, and I was so out of practice.

I waited for the second graders to come in even though the class was Lisa's. They were more likely to catch on to my jokes than kindergartners. Also, funny faces and goofy expressions go over better with a bunch of five-year-olds than jokes did. I read them a book, let them check out their own books, and once they were sitting down I decided it was time to try a joke.

"Who here likes jokes?"

A couple kids raised their hands and a couple silent clapped.

"That's it? Hard crowd. What about if I tell you guys a few jokes? Would you like that?"

They nodded, about half of them with their noses in their books and the rest giving me eye contact.

"What is worse than finding a worm in your apple?"

The kids with books in their hands set them down so they could see me.

They all smiled and giggled with excitement. "What?" they said as a class in unison.

"Finding half a worm."

Silence. Little Angela said, "I don't get it, Mrs. Jones."

"Because if you only find half of the worm and the other half is missing, you don't know where it is. It could still be in the apple you are eating or even in your mouth." I waited for someone to laugh but they just looked at one another and some tilted their heads.

Angela raised her hand, and I pointed at her.

"That is yucky. My mom said when you break a worm in half it becomes two live worms."

Little Johnny with the missing tooth raised his hand next. "Wouldn't you just throw the apple away?"

I thought about that. "I guess you would. Geez, that sounded better in my head, I guess."

"I didn't know worms were in apples. I have one in my lunch, and I'm definitely not eating it," the new girl with the pink glasses said. She crossed her arms in front of her chest, obviously disturbed by my joke.

I was so frustrated. This simple little joke was falling flat, and their parents would probably be calling me to complain because their kids were not going to take a bite of an apple ever again.

"Let me try this again," I said.

This time I had all eyes on me.

"What falls in winter but never gets hurt?"

Johnny raised his hand again. "Leaves."

"No, Johnny," I said. "The leaves fall off the trees in the fall, remember? The trees are bare in the winter."

"I fall in the winter when Emily pushes me," Tommy said. He pushed his thick glasses up.

Oh dear. This was not working out as well as I thought. "It's snow, guys."

Emily frowned and scrunched her eyebrows together. "Snow falls from trees?"

"No. I mean, I guess it could. Guys, snow falls from the sky."

"Oh," they all said together.

"You guys are a tough crowd," I said.

Isabell raised her hand. "Can I go to the bathroom?"

I nodded and watched her run out.

"One more, Mrs. Jones, one more," Johnny said.

I did not want to fall flat on my face again, but what was one more attempt at a good joke to revive myself?

"All right, last one." Remembering my jokes on the spot when every one of them seemed to go over their heads was not easy. "What did the little corn say to the mama corn?"

I saw kids tapping their chins, lost in thought. Little Johnny stared at the ceiling, and Lizzy had her finger up her nose. Emily raised her hand.

"Yes, Emily," I said.

"Let's pop out of here?'

The class erupted in laughs, like hysterical over-dramatized laughs. I could not tell if they were real or not. I cut them off because that was not the answer, and I was pretty sure that little girl just stole my joke.

"The answer is, where is popcorn?"

No one laughed. They just stared at me.

"My big brother says popcorn isn't corn," Johnny said.

"Yeah, I liked Emily's answer better. That was better."

I heard a laugh come from behind me. She-Devil, husband chaser stood behind me.

"I agree. I have one," Lisa Banks said. "What kind of tree fits in your hand?"

Johnny snorted. "What, teacher?"

"A palm tree."

The crowd, including the snobby teacher, all laughed. I cut them off by calling tables to line up at the door. I could not even tell a joke right to seven-year-olds. I was so out of practice.

Lisa walked over to me and whispered, "It's not the joke you tell, it's how you tell it." She rubbed her fingernails on her collar.

And then she had the audacity to wink at me. I stood there stumped. Was that her way of throwing it in my face? Would she ever just be professional and leave me alone? Of course not, that wasn't her style.

HIS TRUCK CAUGHT my attention as it pulled into my driveway right behind me. I stepped out of my car and sighed. I thought about running into my house and locking the door, but knowing Brad, he would not get the hint. He would keep knocking until I gave in and opened the door. I walked inside my house and left the storm door open so I would not have to answer it.

He did a quick knock and opened the door. "Is it okay if I come in?"

"I'm not sure why you're even here," I said.

"Well, I was getting ready to leave and I saw this pink envelope in your mailbox. I thought it might be something important so I figured I'd drop it off on my way ho—to my parent's house."

His parents lived three houses down from ours, which was no longer *our* house, but mine. When we were married, we invested in this small house on the lake with the most breathtaking view of West Sturgeon Lake. My parents helped us with our down payment, and his parents volunteered to help babysit. Brad knew it had been my dream to live on the lake, and we soon remodeled the open floor plan with some help from my father, a retired carpenter. It was our dream house until we split up. Now it was the place I went to hide from the world and be alone with all the pain in my heart. I hated that he was here, uninvited.

I grabbed the letter out of his hand. "Thanks." I turned the envelope over and it said *Don't open until tomorrow morning.*

The last thing I wanted was to see him after work on a Friday when it was supposed to be the start of my weekend, but he was trying to be nice. My ex-husband was my boss, for goodness sake and my neighbor. I was not trying to be rude, but I was never going to escape this guy whether I was at home or work. He would always know where I was and stop by uninvited.

He turned around to leave.

"Brad."

"Yeah?"

"Listen, you have to give me space, okay? Don't ask me how I'm doing. Don't feel bad because I'm a sad, lonely divorcee. Don't act like I'm this delicate flower and tiptoe around me. Just be my boss and treat me like you treat everyone else, okay?"

He nodded. "But you aren't everyone else. What we've been through--"

"I know. But I need this right now, okay?"

He turned to go. "Okay," he said under his breath.

"And Brad."

He held the door open and stared at me with such sadness in his eyes.

"Date who you want. Don't worry about me. We have been done for almost a year now." Saying those words hurt so much, but I had to, even if I did not mean a single word. I had to set boundaries.

With that, he walked out the door, and I stood there watching the spot he had been standing in and staring at me with those sad eyes. His truck squealed out of the driveway, and my heart broke. He needed to have permission to move on with his life, and I needed to move on with mine. The letter in my hand was my first step. I just hoped this one was better than telling jokes to kids. That was a sure way to destroy my self-esteem. I was glad I chose to tell them the jokes in the library instead of the cafeteria, or they would have thrown tomatoes at me, or in their case, apples.

I awoke early the next morning, poured myself a cup of coffee before I carefully opened the pink envelope.

GOOD MORNING SUNSHINE!

If I know you as well as I think I do, you are sitting on your couch in front of your sliding glass door, staring out the window at that breathtaking view of the lake and drinking a cup of hot coffee. Also, I'm sure there is a good book within arm's reach. I know you are nervous about these envelopes, so there is no better way to start than to relax. I will pick you up at nine o'clock this morning, and we are going to the Pebble Spa in Duluth, where we are going to get a double treatment with a sixty-minute massage, foot scrub, and soak, a soothing body brush exfoliation, sauna, tea, and truffles! (Word for word what I read on their website.) You are going to love it. You are desperately in need of some stress relief. Afterward, we are going rock climbing and then out to dinner. Don't forget to pack workout clothes! See you soon. Have I told you how much I've missed you? Although, maybe this is as much for me as it is for you!

. . .

XO WHIT

OKAY, this was not as bad as I thought it would be. A day of relaxation, followed by some exercise and then out to dinner. At the same time, I could not help remembering the last time I went rock climbing. It was back before Ariel was born. Brad and I had the most terrific time. I was terrified of heights, and he stood next to me as we climbed the light-house side-by-side. The lighthouse was a wall on the indoor rock-climbing facility, not a real lighthouse. I almost made it to the top, but my hands were shaking, and my fingers were so stiff. I had two more rocks to reach before I made it to the top, but I could not seem to find a place for my foot. I made the mistake of looking down, and that was when I fell.

Brad dropped down and talked me into getting back up there to finish what I started. I was so disappointed in myself. He gave me a pep talk and a kiss. I clipped myself in and started climbing. I listened to his directions on which hand and foot holds to use. When I pulled myself up that last rock, he clapped and cheered. I was a bit embarrassed at the time about the fuss he was making, but it was a moment I would never forget. I was so proud of myself for beating my fear of heights. We defeated so much together when things were good between us. I could not help but feel a little sad that he was no longer a part of my life.

Whitney arrived right on time, and I met her outside. She had on a red and black checkered flannel over a tank top and yoga pants. It fit in with her whole Paul Bunyan northern Minnesota lumberjack vibe. She greeted me with a hug. Her big smile was very contagious.

"Are you excited?"

I thought about it for a moment. "Yes, I guess I am. I've never been to a spa before."

"You're going to love it! And our day won't be complete without some nineties music, of course."

"Bring on some P-Diddy and Sublime," I said.

We started off with a little TLC, followed by Garth Brooks, Whitney Houston, Backstreet Boys, and my favorite nineties singer, Britney Spears. We were singing as loud as we could and dancing in our seats. The positive memories of our teenage years came back to life in our minds, before we had to grow up and be adults. Drivers in the cars we passed stared at us curiously as we danced in our seats. We even stuck our hands out the sunroof at some point to 'lift the roof'. I forgot what it was like to let it all out and be free and have an excuse to dance however I wanted. To let the music run through my veins and straight to my heart. I experienced a burst of excitement and happiness that pulled the sadness from my soul for a few moments.

As we pulled up in front of the spa, I did not want to get out of the car. I wanted to keep driving. Maybe we could just keep driving to the west coast of California or Oregon even. I did not want this time with my best friend to end. Obviously, we could not drive across the country today, but in my head it was nice to imagine the possibility.

"Oh no, a parking meter. Let's park in back instead. Who knows how long we're going to be here, and I don't want to keep feeding this meter."

We got back into the car, staring ahead at the smaller aerial lift bridge that rises when ships enter the harbor basin from Lake Superior. Canal Park was what I liked to think of as a miniature Manhattan. Sure, Duluth did not have the same population or skyscrapers, or even businesses, but it was where all the fun happened, like concerts, shows, and hockey games at the DECC, brewpubs, galleries, restaurants, and gift shops. There was even a walking path down by the lake with pebble stone beaches and a lake walk for bikers and runners.

In the summertime, people came from all over to run Grandma's Marathon and run the north shore. I loved the view and what it brought in.

We finally found a parking spot behind the building in paid parking. We had a great view of Lake Superior and the giant boat that was anchored beside the smaller blue lift bridge for people to walk over. We got out and walked to the railing by the water. I looked over the edge and closed my eyes as the cold wind blew my blonde hair back and numbed my ears.

Whitney squeezed my hand. "It's moments like this you can feel her with you, can't you?"

"That's exactly what I was thinking," I said. "How did you know that?"

She smiled. "Because I know you."

I took a deep breath and buttoned up my jacket tight as I followed Whitney around the building and into the spa. We waited in comfortable chairs with pretty pillows. Plants and lamps gave the area such a relaxing vibe.

We only had to wait a couple minutes before the masseuse came out to get us, but I almost fell asleep because I was so relaxed in this environment.

We spent the next hour in complete ecstasy. I fell asleep during the foot massage. Brad used to rub my feet while we watched television before going to bed on the weekends. Sometimes we'd rub each other's feet at the same time, both of us relaxed and stress-free after a long day of taking care of Ariel when she was a baby. She was not colicky or moody and she slept through the night straight from the hospital, but sometimes she would get terrible stomach aches. We put a hot water bottle on her belly to help get the bubbles out. How I longed for those days with her. I'd take her screaming at the top of her lungs in exchange for having her back in this world with me again.

I nursed her for the first year, and Brad would always burp her afterward. He was such a good dad and husband, never complaining. We were quite a team. I never understood why my friends' husbands did not share the responsibility for taking care of their children with their spouses. They were, after all, just as much the baby's parent as the mothers.

In northern Minnesota, hunting and fishing are popular sports for men, but some females, too. Brad was one of those men who loved anything outdoors, especially deer hunting. I would rather stay home for some me-time while he was hunting.

For the first three years of our daughter's life, he refused to hunt because he wanted to be home with his family. He worked full-time, and when I protested, he would look at me and say, "Hunting and fishing can wait. There is nothing I want more than to be right here with the two of you." I am pretty sure he never missed hunting season before Ariel was born, for anything. He was a devoted husband and father and at that moment, I fell even more in love with him.

He was nowhere near perfect, and neither was I. Our relationship had its difficulties, but we loved and respected each other. We fought passionately and then made up passionately. We never went to bed angry, and we always kissed first thing in the morning and the last thing before bed. But after the accident, our marriage fell apart. In my heart I know that if I was with them when it happened, our daughter would still be alive. I would have told him to call the police and to move our car farther over to the side of the road. He got out to help someone on the highway and our car was hit by another car driving by. Ariel was in the car because Brad was checking on the other car. It was no one's fault, the police told me. The car was going around a corner and did not see Brad's car, and they could not avoid a collision because another vehicle was next to them in the left lane. I know the driver was sober and luckily not hurt. Hell, he didn't even have a ticket on his record. He was from somewhere in Iowa, driving to Bemidji to visit some friends.

ONCE OUR MASSAGES WERE OVER, we got dressed and walked outside, each of us struggling to put one foot in front of the other.

"How are we going to rock climb now? I'm exhausted," Whitney said. "I probably should have booked the appointment after we went rock climbing instead of the other way around."

Her tongue was hanging out of her mouth and her eyes squinted. Anyone watching would assume she was high, and I felt the way she looked, exhausted, but so relaxed.

"Climbing will be a great way to wake up, and I've been looking forward to climbing again."

"I'm glad one of us feels that way," Whitney said as she opened the door to Adventure Zone where the rock-climbing facility was hidden in the far back corner. "I know you haven't gone since what, before Ariel was born, right?"

I nodded and took in all the changes to the arcade that had been made in the last few years. The laser tag was still there, I was happy to see.

"I can't believe I've never been here before. Brittany would love it here. Hell, I love it here."

"And how long have I begged you to come here with me?"

She smiled. "Way too long. Don't tell me you're afraid of heights."

"Not any more than you are."

"Let's do this."

5

We signed our waivers and paid the employee who looked no older than twenty-one. We rented harnesses and shoes, and our instructor gave us a brief rundown of how to use the equipment. I struggled to get the harness around my waist the right way, and the instructor assisted me. Whitney covered her mouth to hide her laugh as his hand pulled on the strap around my thigh.

"How does that feel?" he said, kneeling before me on the ground.

"Good." I turned away to hide my blush and tried not to make eye contact with Whitney because I knew she would give me a look and I would be unable to hold a straight face.

We followed him through the small chunks of tire that cushioned the ground around the climbing area. The tires gave us a little bounce in our step as we walked.

In front of one of the more difficult walls, he demonstrated how to use the auto belays safely, of course, using me as an example.

"There are twelve auto belays here at Vertical Endeavors

and 14,000 square feet of climbing surface which makes it one of the best-rounded facilities in the Midwest and the North Shore's largest climbing facility. The walls are up to forty-two feet high. Make sure to ring the bells on the front wall when you make it up to the top, and make sure to try my favorite, the lighthouse, which has a hand-carved cliff halfway up the wall."

I stepped back and admired the familiar lighthouse. It was a nice climbing wall for beginners like me.

He looked in my direction and winked. "Any questions?"

"What's your phone number?" Whitney whispered, but it came out too loud, and he smiled at me.

I looked at the ground after he made eye contact with me and tried to act like I never heard a thing.

"Is there something your friend wants to ask me?"

Whitney turned to me. "I don't know, is there something you want to ask him, Madeline?"

My mouth flew open, and my eyes widened. "Nope, I think I'm good." I shot her a warning look.

She laughed. "Don't mind my friend, she's shy."

I slapped her arm, and she yelled out, "What?"

He walked away, and Whitney grinned at me. "He was totally flirting with you."

"Stop, you're terrible," I said.

"He's like twenty-five," she said. She put her hand in the air. "Don't leave me hanging. That is a high five, you sexy cougar. I'm trying to help you out."

I slapped her hand this time. I wasn't going to tell her I thought he in no way looked a day over twenty-one. "Fine, but I'm no cougar. I'm only thirty ... something."

She laughed and led the way to the front wall. We started with the kids' wall with big rocks. Whitney made me go first. I climbed the wall one hand and foot at a time and did not let myself look down or it would all be over. I had two steps to go when my hand started shaking. I had a habit of using my arms more than my legs to pull myself up, so they were quite sore. Once I rang the bell, I jumped back and the rope dropped me to the ground in slow motion.

"You make that look so easy."

I unclipped my harness and clipped it on her belt. "The trick is not to look down. It's always scariest the first time you let go and have to trust the rope will catch you."

She went up about halfway and then dropped to the ground. "You're right. I feel better now that I know the rope can hold me."

She climbed up two more times before she finally rang the bell. As she put both feet on the floor and pulled on the rope, her tongue hung out of her mouth. "That's exhausting. How are we going to do this for a couple more hours?" She nodded in the direction of our instructor just as he glanced at us. "Luckily we have some eye candy to keep us entertained."

The whole time we were rock climbing she teased me about him. "There's your new boyfriend, Maddy," and "Do you want me to see if his mom lets him have a cell phone so you can give him your number?"

I must admit, I loved the attention. He came over and checked that I was clipped in a couple of times, and he smelled and looked like an Abercrombie model. But no, I was not into him, was I? If he had asked me for my number I would like to think I would not have given it to him. He was good looking, but too young for me. Besides, I did not want a relationship right now. I needed to find myself again.

I made it three quarters of the way up the lighthouse but missed the hand hold with my right hand and sprung slowly to the ground. I had blisters on my hands, and my forearms were on fire. I climbed the easy walls up front again and rang the bell. I wanted more than anything to climb the lighthouse, but my strength was low and the climb would be quite difficult. My legs were like rubber, and my grip strength was giving out on me.

Every muscle in my body hurt, including my forearms, abs, even my toes hurt from curling around the rocks. But it was all worth it because I was once again facing my fear of heights and completing climbing challenges I never thought possible. Brad and I used to climb until our grip strength was completely gone and taking off our climbing harness and shoes was a challenge.

WHITNEY TRIED both sides of the lighthouse, but she stopped just short of the height I reached. She was getting better and better.

"It looks so much higher than it is from the top of the wall," she said as she wiped the sweat from her brow.

"I know. I can't stop thinking that the rope is going to break, and I'm going to free-fall to the ground and die."

"I worry more that the auto belay is going to stop working, not so much that the rope will break. Don't worry, I'm sure the young hottie would catch you," she said glancing over her shoulder.

I followed her gaze. "We'd probably both die."

"Maybe you should invite him out for pizza with us."

"Not happening."

"It was worth a try."

We walked a couple buildings over to get pizza. Old Chicago was jumping with people. We split a large deep dish pizza and ate until we were sick. We talked about school and when we first started working together.

"Yesterday was a really good day at school. I love how five-year-olds have no filter and tell you everything. Gayle told me her dad and mom were yelling, and her dad got hauled away in a police car. Another kid argued with her and said she was lying."

"Kids are so honest," Whitney said. "Lillianna told me last week her uncle rode in a police car when he got caught selling grass to his neighbor. Grass. She actually thought it was grass from their lawn, which led to a whole lot more questions from the other kids. I did everything I could not to laugh and I tried to distract them, but they were so worked up about it."

I shook my head. "How about the day Katie told you her parents like to make funny noises, and they have toys in their bedside drawer? That was a fun one."

"I will never forget that day. Kids are so honest at that age. Why aren't we that honest?"

"I'm not sure, but I have to tell you that your first note wasn't exactly good for my self-esteem."

"Comedy with kids? Why? What happened?"

"Well, it didn't go as well as expected." I told her exactly what happened and she laughed so hard she had beer coming out of her nose.

"You have to be kidding me? Kids are so unpredictable."

"I think I may have to rethink my dreams of being a comedian."

"Or you just need to start practicing."

6

I was surprised to find myself sad on Monday morning when a pink envelope was not waiting in my mailbox. By noon I thought maybe it ended up in someone else's mailbox, but after searching all of them, still no envelope. I went into Whitney's room during her prep time, which happened to be my lunch break. To my surprise, I found a man sitting at her desk, busy writing.

"Excuse me," I said. "Where is Whitney?"

He looked at me, confused. "I don't know, I'm just her sub. Is there something I can help you with?"

Something was familiar about this man. I was sure I'd seen him before. Where?

His face brightened, and he stood and walked toward me, crossing his arms in front of him as if he recognized me, too. "Wait a minute. I'd never forget your beautiful face. Were you rock climbing with your friend in Duluth last weekend?"

No, it couldn't be. But yes, I could pick out that crooked smile and broad shoulders anywhere. He was definitely the young, hot, rock-climbing instructor. Where the hell was

Whitney? Was this really happening? How was it even possible?

He squinted at me. "Oh, I'd love to know what you're thinking right now. You're very beautiful, you know that?"

I blushed even more, my palms sweating. "What are you doing here?"

He raised his eyebrows. One side of his mouth formed into a smirk. He knew he was good-looking and cocky about it. I could not hide my annoyance.

"It is a small world, I guess. I'm subbing for this teacher."

"How are you even old enough?"

I shot Whitney a quick text to find out where she was and why she wasn't here. She was not going to believe this.

He took a step closer, obviously testing me. He was definitely too close, and in my bubble. I took a step back and shot him an annoyed glance. "You couldn't be a day over 21."

"Actually, I'm twenty-five. I drive to Duluth for school, and I work at Vertical Endeavors because it helps me stay fit and healthy, and I can climb for free all I want. I just finished my master's degree in elementary education. I have been a sub at the Hibbing schools for a couple of months now."

If he was trying to impress me, it was working. I did not have my masters, but it was on my to-do list. Here he was a decade younger than me and of course he had his.

"I've completed my assistant teaching, just waiting on a job opening. When I got the call about this long-term subbing job for--"

"What do you mean long term? What happened to Whitney?"

I pulled my phone out of my pocket and stared at the screen. Still no text from her. "This has to be a misunderstanding."

"Something about a broken leg," he said.

I ran out of the room without even a goodbye and called

Whitney. I was relieved when someone picked up on the second ring.

"Hello," a sweet little voice said. If I hadn't been so worried about my friend, my heart would have dropped at the sound of her voice. "Brittany? It's Maddy. Is your mom around?"

"She's in surg-wery. Do you want to talk to my dad?"

"Yes, please." I could hardly get the words out. I was pacing back and forth in my classroom, and I could hardly breath. Surgery? What the hell happened?

"Hey, Maddy, it's Josh. Whitney wanted me to wait until after the surgery to call you because she didn't want you to worry."

"What the hell happened?"

He breathed deeply into the phone. "We went biking last night. Whit got distracted and fell off her bike on Redhead and broke her leg. I had to carry her, it was terrible. We went straight to the hospital in Duluth. They said she needed surgery right away. The break was pretty bad, but the doctor says she's going to be okay."

"Is there anything I can do to help?"

"Well, yes, actually, since you asked. Could you take Brittany for a couple days so she doesn't have to miss another day of school? I really hate to ask, but we have no one else."

The thought made me anxious. Take Brittany without Ariel? The idea had me more worked up than my best friend in surgery. Was I that selfish? "Where are Whit's parents?"

"They're in Arizona, and my parents can't come on such short notice."

I closed my eyes. Say no. I'm not ready. Instead I heard myself say, "No problem."

His voice changed. "Really? You don't mind? Are you sure?"

"No problem," I said again. Those words were all I could think of other than how the hell was I going to be okay?

"Thank you, thank you. You're a life saver, you know that? When can you leave? I'll meet you halfway."

I covered my eyes with my free hand. "I can come right after school."

"You're the best. You really are. What would we do without you?"

I could not leave them high and dry, but I regretted agreeing to this. Caring for Brittany would be the hardest thing I'd had to do since Ariel passed away.

I HELD myself together until Lisa came and got her kids, and once again referred to me as Miss Jones. As soon as the last kid left, I lost it. I broke down crying. That one tiny jab put me over the edge. I could not do this. I had to call and let Whitney's husband know I was not ready. Brittany could stay at the hospital, and I would bring her homework if she needed me to, but I could not take care of her. I just couldn't. The pain was just too much.

My tears were like a waterfall that would not turn off. I sat on the floor in the middle of the library with my phone at arm's length. I wanted to pick it up and call or even text and let him know I could not come, but I just stared at it. Would they understand? When would this anger and pain ever end?

I pulled my knees to my chest, wrapped my arms around my legs, and cried.

"Hey, hey, what happened?"

I looked up to find the rock climber looking down at me, worry in his eyes. I jumped to my feet and rubbed away the tears, but my face was still wet, and I couldn't stop the sniffles.

"Just a little breakdown. It's been a long day. You must think I'm crazy."

He grabbed a tissue off my desk and handed it to me. "Did you find out what happened to your friend? Is she okay?"

"She's fine," I said, trying to brush it off.

"Well, there must be some reason why I found you the way I did. Please, is there something I can do?"

I shook my head. If I tried to speak, I would cry. He was the only person in the whole school who did not know about my daughter. He was the only person who did not look at me with pity, like I was fragile. Although, I may have just changed that. I gathered my things, ready to make a break for it. I had to go.

"I have five sisters," he said.

"Excuse me?" Did I hear him right?

"I just mean, if you ever want to talk, I'm here. That's all. I'm good with girl problems. I'm next door that is, if you change your mind."

For the first time since I met him, he did not look cocky at all. He looked kind, maybe even vulnerable.

"And you can call me Tim."

"Tim?"

"That's my name."

"Oh, well, see you tomorrow, Tim …"

He turned around to look at me. "Thank you."

He nodded and I turned before he could say anything in return. I could do this. I was not that broken. Was I?

7

Loud music and a long, relaxing drive gave me the strength to do what I needed to do. I could not let my best friend down. I told Josh not to meet me halfway because I wanted to see Whitney, and I did not want him to leave his wife all alone. She had no one else, and she needed me. I had to put my emotions aside for the next couple of days.

By the time I drove into the hospital parking lot, Whitney was awake and sitting up in bed. Her eyes lit up when she saw me. "Maddy, you're here."

"Maddy!" Brittany came running to me. I wrapped her in my arms and picked her up. Her sweet hug melted my heart. What was I so scared of?

"Are you here to pick me up for the sleepover?"

Energy and excitement was radiating through her. I squeezed her little cheek and she giggled. "Aren't you the cutest?" I pulled her in again because I couldn't get enough of her hugs.

"Britt, I'd like a glass of water. Why don't you take daddy to the waiting room down the hall."

Josh nodded.

Once they were gone, she pushed the button on her bed so she sat up taller.

Her leg was in a full cast. "How's the leg?"

"The good thing is I can't feel it with all the drugs they have me on."

"Well, that's good," I said.

Her expression changed to concern. "Are you sure you're okay taking her for a few days? Josh should have talked to me before he asked you. I hope he didn't make you feel pressured into taking her. You've been through a lot, and I understand if you can't do it. Men are so clueless sometimes."

"It's fine. I missed her and I'm excited to spend some time with her. You just worry about getting better, okay?"

She nodded her head. Her eyes kept closing. She was forcing her body to stay awake to make sure I was okay. She wanted to talk more about how I was feeling, but she needed her sleep so I had to cut her off. I needed to be there for her. She was my best friend, and she never asked me for anything.

Her eyes opened, and I reached for her hand.

"How can I leave you the daily letters when I'm stuck in this hospital?"

I smiled. "I think I will have my hands full for now. You just worry about getting better, okay?"

She closed her eyes.

I CARRIED HER SUITCASE, sleeping bag, and pillow inside my house and set them down on the living room floor. Brittany followed me in with her unicorn pillow pet and teddy bear. She was rubbing her eyes.

"Will you read me a story like you used to do when I'd come and play with Ariel?"

That was the first time I heard my daughter's name from Brittany's mouth since she left this world.

"Sure."

She took off with her teddy bear and pillow in hand before I could call her back. I saw her shadow down the hall as she opened Ariel's squeaky door. I ran to catch her before she did any damage.

"Sweetie, let's not go in there. Britt, Brittany!"

By the time I reached my daughter's door, Brittany was on the floor by Ariel's bookshelf, grabbing Pete the Cat books.

"One," I said sternly. Her eyes darted up to mine with a bit of confusion.

How dare she run into this room without even asking? I had to leave the room for a minute before I lost it. "Okay, pick out two books and put your pj's on. I'll be back in a couple minutes. I walked outside, did some deep breathing, and once I felt like I would not lose it on this six-year-old, I opened the door.

My phone buzzed in my hand from an unknown number. I don't usually answer the phone when I don't know the number, but answering it would be a good distraction from having to go back into that room.

"Hello," I said.

"Hey Maddie, it's Tim."

I searched my brain, but I was pretty sure I had not known a Tim since high school. "Tim who?"

"Tim the rock-climbing instructor turned substitute teacher that you can't get enough of," he said with a laugh.

I looked at my phone and then placed it back on my ear. "Oh, that Tim. How did you get this number?"

"The principal gave me the directory. I'm not a stalker, I swear. I just wanted to make sure you were okay. I hated the way you left today, and I couldn't live with myself if I didn't at least check on you."

"Well, thanks but I'm a little busy right now."

"I understand. I'm sorry I called. I couldn't help myself."

Now I felt like a jerk. He seemed so concerned over the phone, a different person than the young confident stud I met at the rock-climbing place.

"That's kind of ... sweet, but you don't have to worry about me, okay? I do appreciate you checking on me though."

"You think I'm sweet?"

Just when I thought maybe he wasn't as cocky as he came off, he had to make a comment like that. "Goodbye, Tim."

"No, wait!"

I hung up. Too late. I did not have time for Tim and his ego.

I walked back into Ariel's room, ready to tell Brittany she had to sleep in the guest room, but she was curled up on Ariel's bed, fast asleep. I imagined for just a second that Ariel was in the bed. My heart broke at the thought.

I leaned against the doorframe and watched as the little girl's chest rose and fell with each gentle breath. I moved a little closer and peeked at her sweet face. How lucky she was to have a long life ahead of her. If only Ariel had the same opportunity. I knew it wasn't Brittany's fault she was alive and my Ariel wasn't, but I could not help but feel jealous, and I hated that I felt this way. Hopefully this was only for a night or two because this was just too much for me.

BRITTANY WAS awake before me the next morning. She came running into my room and started jumping on my bed. I grabbed her and pulled her down, tickling her. She giggled with big belly laughs as she kicked her feet and tried to get away.

When I stopped, she called out, "Again, again!"

I climbed off the other side of the bed. "We have to get up and make breakfast and get ready for school."

"What are we having?"

"How about blueberry pancakes?"

"Yes!"

She raced to the breakfast bar and climbed up, nearly tipping the stool over.

"Careful," I said, pulling my robe over my shorts and tank top.

"Do you know why I'm sitting in Ariel's spot?"

I held my breath as I waited for her to go on. I had to let her finish. If I said no, I would be rude and hurt her feelings and she would probably end up telling me anyway. Instead I said, "Why?"

"Because I miss her, and I want to be just like her. My mom said she is with the angels in heaven. Do you think she's happy there? Do you think she misses us?"

Her words were a way to get my blood flowing rapid first thing in the morning. I hoped my daughter was in a place better than this one, but the truth was, when she died I stopped believing in heaven and God. Why would God take my baby from me? No god would do that. He would have saved her.

I tickled her belly button. "I think she's happy, but I'm sure she would rather be here with us."

She wrapped her arms around her chest and smiled at me.

"I think she misses you and her daddy, too. I think she has pink wings, and she lives in a castle with a crown and a long pink dress. I think every day she looks down on us from her magical ball and wishes she could play with us again."

"Wow, you've really thought about this, huh?"

She nodded. She used so many hand gestures as she

talked, and now she was dancing around the kitchen like a ballerina.

She stopped suddenly and said, "You know she has a princess name for a reason, right? They needed more princess angels in heaven."

She had a good point and more of an idea as to why she left us than I did. I only wished I could have as much faith in what we cannot see. If only for a moment, it made me smile to think of her as a princess angel in heaven, flying around with pink sparkly wings.

I PUT up spring decorations all around my library on my lunch hour and prep hour. I printed a ton of coloring sheets and even bought some new crayons for the kids. I probably spent a couple hundred dollars of my own money on them, but most teachers did. The budget was tight and parents were only asked to help out so much. Even specialty classes like art, gym, and music were cut down to a third of the year.

Tim knocked softly, but did not wait for a reply before walking in.

"Why hello, beautiful. Getting all set up for spring?"

"Trying," I said.

"Can I give you a hand?"

I loved that Whitney and I always had the same prep time because we would help each other with decorations, but I wished Tim would let me be. No one could ever replace Whitney, but I did need the help.

"I have a feeling if I say no you'll stick around chatting anyway so sure, might as well keep you busy. The bunnies and eggs need to be cut out on that table if you don't mind. I've turned on the laminator so they'll need to be laminated once they're cut out.

He looked at me nervously. "Don't laugh at me, but I've never used a laminator before."

I laughed anyway and shook my head. "It's actually pretty easy. Here, let me show you."

He followed me to the table and stood so close I smelled a mixture of his cologne and tangerine, maybe? Whatever it was, he smelled so good I had to breathe out of my nose just to keep pleasuring my senses. I opened up the plastic and placed the word spring inside. I helped to guide it through the machine, and he watched carefully. He leaned in, our heads almost touching. He stared at me, and a tingle coursed through my body. He placed his fingers next to mine to help guide the paper through the machine. When we touched, I felt a shock and pulled away to let him finish on his own.

"You okay?"

I walked back to the table and hung up the completed decorations. "I'm fine. Thank you for helping, but I think I've got it from here."

He laminated the artwork and did not act as though he heard me trying to get rid of him. Why was he making me so nervous? I felt like a silly schoolgirl.

I heard another knock and in walked my ex-husband. Really? I dared not look up as I hung the art.

"I'm here on official principal business," Brad said. "I'm letting all the teachers know we're having a fire drill tomorrow."

"Thanks," I said, still not giving him eye contact.

He stood there, staring at my back as I grabbed the word spring and hung it up.

"How's Whitney doing? Have you talked to her?"

"Yeah, she seems to be doing okay."

He bent over and put his hand on mine, and stared at me until I had to look up.

Of course, Tim decided that was a great time to clear his

throat and make his presence known from behind Brad. Should I be grateful at that moment or annoyed? I wasn't sure.

"Oh, Mr. Admonson, I didn't see you there. You two are ..."

Brad sounded nervous. Caught off-guard.

"Just thought I'd give Maddy a hand," Tim said. A huge smirk spread across his face at his stupid joke.

He was going to give me so much crap for this. I could see it in his eyes.

Brad's poise changed, his shoulders went back, and his back straightened. "How are you liking teaching kindergarten?" His voice deepened with his words.

"It's not bad. I think I could get used to it."

He was obviously holding back a laugh.

Brad crossed his arms and pushed out his chest. "That's great."

Was he trying to intimidate him? Challenge him?

"Maddy here has been very welcoming," Tim said with a shit grin.

Brad's face turned red, and I had to do everything I could to keep from laughing. Tim was enjoying this way too much. What did he know exactly?

"Is she? Well, that's great. I'll let you two get back to it."

Brad left so fast I was in shock. I stood up.

"That was hilarious. I've changed my mind. You're welcome in here anytime."

"It is pretty obvious your boss has a huge crush on you. Did you see the way he looked at me when he saw I was there and saw him touch you?"

Here Tim thought he was making a big discovery. Should I tell him the truth or keep playing with him? The truth would only lead to more questions, and only a matter of time before I'd have to tell him about Ariel and the divorce. But I liked that everything was simple with him.

"You think so? I never noticed."

Tim sure had Brad going. I loved the jealous look Brad had when he saw Tim was there, although I would never admit it. Was it jealousy or the shock of being caught? It didn't matter, either way he was shaking in his boots. I seldom saw Brad that way. Maybe Tim wasn't so bad after all.

8

"She is so happy, Maddy. I can't thank you enough," Whitney said.

She had just spoken with Brittany on the phone. Now Brittany was playing with Ariel's dollhouse, and I was watching her like a hawk to make sure she didn't accidentally break anything.

"I still can't believe my sub messed with Brad like that, by the way. I can only imagine what Brad thought. Oops."

She seemed to have a little more energy today, but she was obviously holding back as she laughed, due to the pain.

"I will find a way to keep getting you those letters. Time is running out, and summer vacation will be here before we know it."

"I know you're bummed about not having letters for me right now, but I'm doing pretty good at making myself laugh on my own and don't worry we've still got a lot of time before the end of the school year for you to boss me around."

"Stop making me laugh. It hurts," she said. "How is Brittany? Has she been behaving herself? She sounded really happy on the phone."

"She's been doing really well. She misses you guys, though. When will you be out of the hospital?"

"I should be out by the end of the weekend. The doctor still has some concerns, and I have one more surgery coming up tomorrow, but Monday at the latest. So what does this sub look like? Is he hot?"

I heard Josh in the background say, "Hey!"

"Oh stop. What do you have to be worried about?" Whitney said. "It's not like your wife is going anywhere. You think I could pick up guys like this? Really?"

"I didn't tell you who he is?" I said.

"What are you talking about? Do I know him? I don't think I know any male subs that would be crazy enough to take on kindergartners."

I was so busy I forgot to tell her who Tim was.

"He's--"

"Maddy, hold that thought. The doctor is here and he needs to speak with me. Talk tomorrow?"

I was so disappointed. She was not going to believe who he was, and it might take some convincing for her to believe me. "Yeah."

"Give my baby kisses for me, and Maddy, thank you. I owe you one."

I found Brittany in Ariel's room playing Barbies. The dolls were in an old briefcase stored under her bed so she could reach them easily. Ariel would sit in her room for hours doing their hair and playing pretend with them. She had the pink Barbie convertible and a minivan that could fit eight Barbies in it. Some of the Barbies had jagged haircuts from Ariel practicing her beauty skills. I'd find Barbie hair hidden in backpacks and shoved into drawers when I'd help her clean her room. The first time I found a wad of hair I thought she was cutting her own hair, but after yelling at her I realized it wasn't her hair. I even found pieces of her clothes cut up.

"Mama, I was designing clothes," she said once in her sweet, innocent little voice. "I'm sorry, mama, but that shirt was too small for me anyway," she said another time. How do you even argue with that?

WHEN SHE WAS ABOUT THREE, she cut off her bangs. She came running out of her room with her hair in her hand. "Mama, look how pretty!"

Brad and I exchanged big eyes and nervous glances. He turned his back so she could not see him hold in his smirk, while I sternly lectured her. She kept grinning the whole time I lectured her. She thought she did such a great job. Boy was she a spitfire.

I searched the house for scissors and put them up high in case she got any more ideas.

Opening the door to Ariel's room and having someone enjoy the toys Ariel once enjoyed so much actually felt good. A feeling that surprised me. Before I wanted to shut it all away so the pain wouldn't be so intense, but this was feeling better than I expected.

Brittany turned her head and smiled brightly at me. "Will you play with me?"

Before I could turn her down, she handed me the Ariel Barbie with long red hair and a mermaid tail. I stared at it and then I figured, why not? I got down on my knees and placed Ariel in the convertible.

"Maddy, she can't drive, she doesn't even have feet!" Then she let out the biggest belly roar. "You are silly."

"Oh, you think that's funny, huh? Well she can't do much since there isn't any water for her to swim in," I said. What would she have to say to that?

She shook her head. "It's pretend. The water is pretend."

That's the thing about kids. Not only were they great at using their imaginations, they were great at changing the rules so parents never won. Ariel ended up marrying Ken, and I grabbed some confetti from my craft room to throw in the air as they swam down the aisle.

Brittany's giggle was catchy, and we both laughed and laughed. Then we made chocolate chip cookies, and I taught her how to prepare homemade lasagna for dinner. She could not see over the counter, so I pulled Ariel's old pink stepping stool out of the closet and washed off the dust.

Like Ariel, she tried to steal cookie dough, and I had to lecture her on salmonella poisoning and tell her the story of how Brad ended up in the hospital after eating a spoonful of cookie dough.

"One time my momma was making a cake and my daddy put a spoonful of frosting in his mouth. My mom stayed quiet, and then he spit it out in the garbage cause it was lard."

"Your mom never told me about that. That's really funny," I said. "I can totally see your dad doing that." How did she even know what lard was?

"Why don't you love Brad anymore?"

Her question was so out of the blue, it shocked me. She was probably the only person who could get away with asking me that question, but I was at a total loss how to answer it.

"Sometimes mommies and daddies just don't love each other anymore," I said hoping she would drop it.

"Do you think my mommy and daddy are going to stop loving each other like you and Brad?"

The look in her eyes broke my heart. "No, I don't think so. You see when Ariel went to heaven, Brad and I were really sad, and we thought if we didn't live together we might be happier."

She stared up at me with those beautiful sparkly blue eyes. I could see another question coming my way.

"Are you?"

"Are we what?"

"Happier?"

I thought about it. Was I happier? "I don't know," I said honestly. "What I do know is that I am happier now that you are here." And I truly meant it from the bottom of my heart. I was lighter somehow with her around.

She leaned her head closer to me and puckered her lips. I bent down, and she kissed my cheek and hugged my neck with her cookie dough hands, but I did not care because I was happy right there in that moment. I did not want her to leave, ever. Why had I been so scared to have her come stay with me?

The cookies and lasagna were a perfect end to our night, followed by a bubble bath in my jacuzzi tub with lots of bubbles and jets. I even let her bring Ariel into the bath with her. We laughed, and I taught her some songs from my childhood that I always sang with Ariel. My cheeks actually hurt from laughing so hard by the time I toweled her off.

We read a story together and as I reached for the light switch, I heard, "Maddy?"

"Yes, sweet girl."

"I love staying at your house. Can I live here with you?"

I laughed and sat down at the edge of her bed. "I really wish you could, but don't you think your mommy and daddy would be really sad?"

She tapped her chin with her pointer finger. "Yeah, I guess they would. You just seem so lonely in this house all by yourself."

I got up to leave. "I'm okay. Don't you worry about me. Get some sleep, okay?"

"Hey, Maddy."

I turned around. "Yes?"

"I love you."

"I love you, too."

I LITERALLY JUMPED out of bed the next morning at five a.m. I put on my workout clothes, walked on my treadmill in the basement for thirty minutes, cooked omelets for breakfast with a side of strawberries, and jumped in the shower quick before Brittany woke up. It was Wednesday, and I couldn't wait to go to school. We ate breakfast and brushed our teeth together. We had a hard time picking out an outfit that Brittany wanted to wear, but settled on pink unicorn leggings and a purple matching unicorn shirt. She let me braid her hair like I did so many times for Ariel. Ariel's hair was much thicker, but Brittany's hair was so much easier to braid.

"I was thinking this weekend we could go to the aquarium in Duluth if your mom is still in the hospital."

"What's the quarium?"

"Hasn't your mom taken you there?"

She shook her head.

"It's a place where all kinds of animals and mammals live and people get to visit. You're going to love it. It's in Duluth."

"I love animals! Do they have electric eels there? I always wanted to see one."

"You know what? I think they do."

She climbed out of her chair and danced around the kitchen. I took her hand and spun her and then dipped her. We giggled and rubbed our noses together before I stood her back up.

"Okay, it's time for school," I said. "Grab your backpack, and I'll get your lunchbox."

I walked her to her classroom on the other end of the building, gave her a hug and kiss, and went on to unlock the library. I had just hung up my jacket when Tim walked in behind me.

"Hey there, beautiful."

I turned my back to him. "Hi, Tim."

"I was thinking that maybe I could talk you into a movie tonight."

I gave him a disapproving look, and he raised his hands in response as if to say he meant no harm.

"Just as friends. I don't really know anyone in this town or in this school, and I thought it would be nice to get to know you better. Maybe you could even give me some tips on how to survive in this school."

I smiled.

"Look at that, I made you smile. You have beautiful teeth you've been hiding, you know that?"

Here he was in a sweater vest and damn he looked good. The blue brought out the blue in his eyes. From his build, he obviously had a gym membership and for the first time, I wondered what he looked like with his shirt off. The thought had me sweating.

He looked down at his shirt as if to see what I was staring at. "Do I have something on my shirt?"

I glanced away. "I can't go to a movie tonight."

"Oh, come on." He took a step toward me. "Don't tell me you're married because I don't see a ring."

I looked down at my bare hand, and I felt the pain in the pit of my stomach. I hid my hands behind my back.

"It's not that."

He took another step closer. "Do you have a boyfriend?"

He ran his fingers through his John Stamos hair. Now that I thought about it, he really looked a lot like John Stamos. I had a crush on him as a kid when I watched *Full House*. Stamos only got hotter as he got older. I had a feeling Tim had the same fate.

"You think the only reason I would say no is because I have a boyfriend or a husband, huh?"

He raised his eyebrows and for some reason it made me blush. What did this guy have over me? He was so young, and he wasn't really my type. Not that I had a type, but I was just never attracted to cocky men. I had been married so long I never thought about men except my husband in that way in years. Sure, I thought guys were attractive, but none compared to Brad. He stole my heart years ago, and I wanted no one else.

"Tell me you want me to stay away, and I'll quit asking. Give me one reason why you won't go out with me."

"I'm watching my friend Whitney's daughter. You know the one you're subbing for. She's still in the hospital in Duluth so I'm babysitting."

He stepped even closer to me, and he gently took my arm. My knees collapsed beneath me, and he caught me and held me in his arms.

"Careful," he whispered.

He leaned a little closer, just a whisper away, and my lips trembled at the thought of him so close to me. I licked my lips, then looked into his eyes and caught him staring back at me with a look of desire.

"If her daughter wasn't staying with you, you would say yes?"

He placed his hands on the back of my neck, then kissed me lightly on the lips. We pulled away, and I slowly opened my eyes to meet his. He kissed me again with such passion, it took my breath away.

"Maddy?"

I jerked my head away. Brad was standing in the doorway, staring at us. He looked broken. How could I let this happen? Here of all places? Anyone could have walked in. A child, a parent, my ex-husband. Too late.

"I was just--," Tim said.

"I came to ta-ta-talk to you about the fire drill," Brad said. This was so awkward.

I swallowed and managed to say, "What about the drill?"

I needed to keep the conversation going. It was the only thing that separated us from awkward silence.

"It will be at nine this morning," he said. Then he was gone.

Tim eyed me curiously. "Are you sure the two of you aren't dating?"

"Definitely not."

9

"You said no? You deserve this. Hell, you need this. That hot rock-climbing guy, come on! That's it, Josh needs to come home anyway to get some clothes and check on the house. He can leave me alone one night so you can go on a date!"

"No, it's fine. Really. It's no big deal. I don't even know if I'm ready for that. Really."

"Too bad. He was planning on coming home for one night anyway. I should be discharged Monday, and my surgery is tomorrow. I still can't believe you kissed the rock-climbing guy! Why didn't you tell me he was your sub? What are the odds?"

"I tried telling you, but you had a lot going on. I feel bad about Brad though. He looked so angry."

"Oh, honey, the two of you were married for how long. Of course he's going to be jealous. Don't you worry about him. You're coming back to life again, I can see it. You need this distraction."

"It's not like that. Tim is a baby in his mid-twenties. The odds of anything serious stemming from a date or two are slim to none. But please don't have Josh come home on my account. I don't need to go on a date. I don't even know how to date. Hell, I thought I would never date again," I said.

Not long ago, I was praying I'd get some terrible disease that would take me in my sleep so I could be with my girl again. I was not planning on killing myself or anything, just some kind of accident that would stop the constant pain in my heart. This was a welcoming distraction. It felt good to be wanted, maybe even desired by someone so damn good looking and quite technically out of my league.

"Maybe a distraction with someone you don't intend to have a long term relationship is what you need. Girl, you need to get laid."

"That is not what this is. I'm not having sex with him."

"I'm just saying, you may feel better. Anyway, no more arguing, Josh is coming home. Brittany needs him, and he really wants to spend some one-on-one time with her anyway. Problem solved."

"I don't know if I'll go out with him," I said. "He's not my type."

"He's hot and sweet and so into you. What's not your type?"

The whole incident did not stop Tim and me from having lunch together and chatting during our prep time. I showed him where Whitney's Easter and spring decorations were in the cupboard, and we put them up exactly the way she did.

"So tell me how you and Whitney became friends. Did you meet working here?"

He was standing on the back counter while I handed him the decorations to hang up.

"Well, we were in college and I was dating Brad at the time." As soon as I said his name, I wanted to take it back.

"Brad, huh? Where is this Brad now?"

I am a terrible liar, so I was glad he was not looking at me when he asked. Instead of answering him, I said, "Will you just let me tell you the story?"

"Sorry, continue."

"My boyfriend and I came home for the county fair. I wanted to go on the double Ferris wheel, but he refused to go on rides because of how fast the traveling fairs put them up. Anyway, I got in line, and Whitney was also riding by herself so they shoved the two of us on the ride together. Little did we know we know the ride would end up being a very traumatic experience for both of us. The wheel ended up sparking, and the wires shorted and started on fire. And here we were, two strangers stuck on the top. She was petrified and holding on for dear life, so I took the opportunity to tell her some jokes and got her laughing."

"Aren't you afraid of heights? I'm pretty sure I heard you say that when you were rock climbing."

"I am, but I had to stay calm to help her so in the process it calmed me. We helped each other."

"Sounds like you are both pretty great people to me. I can see why you're so close. Sharing a story like that is pretty powerful."

"We also found out we both went to UMD, but we'd never met on campus."

"The two of you went to the same college and you met here, in your home town?"

"Yes, weird, right? It was definitely meant to be. Anyway, we were both going to school for elementary education, and we became study buddies. After a life-or-death situation at a carnival like that, you bond rather quickly. Like you said, it really brings two people together."

"She seems pretty great. I hope I get to meet her one day."

I smiled. "She is. The two of us have been through a lot together."

"I bet you can't wait for her to come back so I'm not bugging you every day."

He shot me that killer smile, and I batted my eyelashes like a teenager. Boy was I smitten with this guy. "I like when you bug me." Did I really just say that? What was I, a sixteen year-old boy crazy teenager or something?

He jumped down from the counter and grabbed my hand. "That's good because I really like bugging you."

"I talked to Whitney last night."

We dropped hands, and he picked up the extra decorations. "How's she doing?"

"She's good. She has surgery this afternoon, and her husband is coming home to see Brittany, and he plans on taking her for the night so ..."

He lifted my chin when I did not finish. "Miss Jones, are you asking me out on a date?"

I picked at my nails. "Maybe."

"Sorry, I was planning on washing my hair," he said with a smirk. "So I'm not sure I'll be able to."

"You're impossible." I threw up my arms and started walking away, but he grabbed my arm and pulled me to him.

I wanted him to kiss me again. Our first kiss was not long enough, and I couldn't stop thinking about it, but the kiss needed to happen somewhere else this time. In school was too risky.

"I'll surprise you with the most amazing date you have ever been on. It is going to blow you away."

"That's a lot of pressure you're putting on yourself," I said. "And I'm not easily impressed. Are you sure you can live up to those expectations?" My heart fluttered at the thought. I bit my lower lip. The way he looked at me, so deep into my eyes, made me feel special.

"I'm always up for a challenge," he said. "I wish I could kiss you right now."

I felt exactly the same way, but I just smiled and walked away.

IT WAS NOT until lunch on Friday I ran into Brad again. Lisa was lecturing me in the mailroom about my mail being mixed with her mail, and that's when I saw the pink envelope in her hand.

"Can I please have my mail?" I said.

"Ugh, I am so sick of getting your mail. If you don't start picking up your mail before your mailbox is full, I'll start throwing your mail in the garbage, you hear me?"

She was not worth arguing with. "Yes, ma'am," I said.

Brad was on his way into his office. He avoided my eyes, and addressed Lisa. "Thanks for all your help organizing the spring carnival. Let me know if I can help with anything."

Lisa's face lit up at the sight of Brad. She glanced my way, then moved closer to Brad.

"I'm having a couple teachers over tonight for dinner. I'm making my grandmother's sarmas if you happen to be in the neighborhood."

He looked at me. I looked away and walked out of the office, but not before hearing him say, "I can swing by."

If he was trying to hurt me back, it worked. I did not want to be with him anymore, but why did he have to choose Lisa? We hated Lisa. He knew the way she treated me, and he knew how upset I was that she was always chasing him when we were dating and even after we were married.

My biggest flaw was to overthink EVERYTHING. I was that annoying person who stressed about things I said that no one even remembered, or the person who hung onto something that was said to me or about me for way too long. I annoyed myself with this. Sometimes I couldn't even sleep, I worried so much. But since the accident, what was said didn't bother me as much, nor did I care what others thought of me. Life was too short to worry about the little things. But with Brad and Lisa, overthinking came back worse than ever. Why did I let her do this to me? Why?

Once I was safely back in my room, I opened the envelope. It was obviously Whitney's envelope, but different handwriting. Male handwriting. I opened it up.

MADDY,

WHITNEY ASKED me to write you this letter since she is unable. She said your task is to take yourself shopping and buy a new outfit at Moxie for tonight. Not sure what this is all about, but she just told me where she kept her envelopes in her desk and that this needed to be put in your mailbox ASAP. Have fun. Whatever you are buying a new outfit for.

Sincerely,
Beth

BETH WAS the gym teacher and a good friend of ours. Whitney went out of her way to make sure I would go through with a date with Tim tonight. I guess I had no choice but to go to Moxie and buy myself a new outfit or maybe even a dress.

I LOVED Moxie and was so excited to find a gorgeous black dress that showed my curves. I took my time with my makeup and straightened my hair. But all I thought about the whole time was images of Lisa and Brad hanging out and drinking, talking about me. I hated the thought of her with him, friends or a couple. Even if she did say there were other teachers coming over, they probably weren't. It was just another trick to get him alone. The thought made me ill.

Twice I started texting Tim to cancel, but then I erased the text. I did not want to be a dud all night, but I had a feeling I would be. I was just so nervous and distracted. I saw the pink envelope on my nightstand, which reminded me why I couldn't cancel. I promised Whitney.

Tim picked me up at quarter to six. His eyes checked out my every curve to the point of me going back into the house to get a shawl because I felt naked. Maybe my bare shoulders were too much? I just wanted to look good, for me. Maybe a little for him, too.

I did not feel the butterflies in my stomach that I usually had when he was around. Maybe because my mind was stuck on other things. He was such a gentlemen, opening doors and shutting them behind me.

We arrived at the Whistling Bird, and I was impressed. The lighting was dim and the tables so private. The Jamaican vibe was the next best thing to paradise. The drinks were tropical and brightly colored and after much debating, I chose a Mai Tai and Tim had a Dirty Banana, which he let me try. His drink was delicious and tasted like a chocolate shake. We both had the coconut shrimp and baby red potatoes. I ate so much I thought I would rip my dress. The food was satisfying, and it distracted me from my toxic thoughts.

"Tell me about your family," I said.

He finished chewing and wiped his face with his napkin. "My mom and dad live on the North Shore. They have a house overlooking Lake Superior. My dad loves to fish, and my mom likes to tag along and relax in the boat reading Colleen Hoover novels."

My eyes lit up. "I'm a huge CoHo fan. I can't believe she got famous from BookTok. That is just unreal and amazing.

Even the top publishing houses are keeping an eye on TikTok now. It's really inspiring."

He nodded. "I didn't realize that."

"What else do your parents like to do?"

"They like to hike, and my dad comes up during hunting season and we go out in the deer stand and hunt together. I think he mainly does it for my benefit now. I'm the one who always ends up shooting the deer. We have a hunting shack just north of where you live."

"Really? I didn't realize that."

"Yep, over by Stoney Brook on the Snake Trail. What is it that you live on? I don't know Side Lake real well."

"I'm on West Sturgeon. As you saw, Turtle Creek Road, the road I live on, is a dirt road on the end of a dead end street. We don't get the traffic like they do on other roads in the summer. It's kind of peaceful."

"It looks like it. I have always wanted to live on a lake. Maybe someday. Probably not on a teacher's salary though." He laughed.

"True," I said. He probably wondered how I afforded it, and I prayed he would not ask.

"You must have gotten a great deal on your place."

I just smiled.

"Now tell me about your family."

How was I going to answer that question? I was not ready to tell him about Ariel, and I felt like I had already lied about Brad. I loved that he knew nothing about me. I could be whoever I wanted to be with him. "Well, my parents passed away when I was twenty-one. It's just me, really."

"Were you ever married?"

"I was, but I'm divorced now."

He looked surprised. "I didn't realize that. We don't have to talk about it if you don't want."

Oh, thank god.

"Let's not ruin the night," I said.

Then he asked the one question I feared the most. "And you don't have any kids, do you?"

I stood up and ran to the bathroom without a word. I hugged my stomach because he knocked the wind right out of me. I could not answer his question, and all I wanted was to go home and curl into a ball on my bed and cry.

I wiped the tears away, splashed some water on my warm cheeks, and walked back out to the table.

"Sorry about that. I'm not feeling well. Can you please take me home? It must have been the shrimp."

10

He let me be the whole way home. I rested my head against the window and hugged my stomach.

"Let me know if you need me to pull over," he said as soon as we got into the car.

When he pulled into my driveway, I opened up the door and ran into my house without another word. I heard him call my name, but I kept running. I did not bother to lock the door.

"Maddy, are you okay?"

I was in my bedroom changing out of the dress that was suffocating me, and he was in my living room. Why couldn't he just go away?

"I'm going to wait for you on your couch. I don't want to leave when you're this ill. Let me know if I can get you anything."

This wonderful, handsome man was waiting for me in my living room, and here I was having a nervous breakdown because I had no idea how to answer the simple question, Do you have kids? I took down most of our family pictures so at least they weren't still up around the house and lead to more questions.

After my divorce, I packed away almost all the pictures of Brad. I could not bear to dwell on my past with him or how upset I was for not protecting Ariel. I put my pictures of Ariel under my bed because it hurt too much to look at all I lost. I did not want to forget her, I just needed a little time. I didn't want to cry every time I passed her pictures in the hallway or stared at them while I tried to forget by watching television.

I went downstairs to politely tell him he needed to go. He was not in the living room. I peeked out the window, but his car was right where he parked it. "Tim?"

"In the kitchen."

I rounded the corner to find him elbows deep in my sink. He hardly turned to look at me as he did the dishes.

"Are you seriously doing my dishes right now?"

He pulled the drain and grabbed a towel off the oven. "I'm sorry, I knew you were going through something and nothing I could do would help you. I felt as though the least I could do was help by cleaning up a little." He looked away. "Who am I kidding, I get terrible anxiety and keeping busy makes me feel better. You must think I'm crazy."

"You're worried I think you're crazy? I go running away after dinner and demand you bring me home before we're even done with our drinks, and you think you're the crazy one?"

He wrinkled his eyebrows, then his face softened, and he shot me his sexy white smile and moved closer to me.

"You aren't like any woman I've ever known."

"Probably because you're still in your twenties."

He laughed. "Age doesn't matter. I know you've been through something, and I want you to know I won't ask you a bunch of questions. When you're ready to talk, I'm here."

"I don't know you well enough, Tim. I mean we just went on our first date."

"Oh, so that was a date."

He caught me off guard and I stared at him sideways.

"Kidding," he said, before I had a chance to panic and overreact and overanalyze his words.

I punched his shoulder playfully, and he held onto it as if I hurt him.

I pushed at his chest. "Oh, stop."

He wrapped his arms around me and pulled me into him again.

I relaxed in his arms.

He pulled me in and kissed me like I'd never been kissed before.

I could not help but compare his lips to Brad's, even if it was wrong. I only knew the passion I had shared all those years with Brad. This was different and it made me giddy. Once he pulled away my bashful smile was hard to hide.

"There is something about you, Miss Jones. I'll see you at school Monday morning. Before you have a chance to tell me again why you don't think this will work."

Was I that easy to read?

He grabbed his coat off the couch and walked out the door. I shut the door behind him and peeked at him through the curtains.

I did not have a lot of experience with men, but it was refreshing to meet someone like Tim. When he came into my house I figured he was here for one reason and one reason only. Since my teen years, I believed that men only wanted one thing. I had a hard time believing Tim might be different. Especially since I was ten years older than him.

. . .

BRITTANY CAME BACK SATURDAY NIGHT. I spent the day cleaning the house, doing laundry, and even made it out for a ten-mile bike ride in the woods. Josh said he was expecting Whitney to be home on Monday, but it would be up to six weeks before she could even return to work so she would probably not be coming back to teach until next year.

BRITTANY WAS NOT HER NORMAL, energetic self.

"How about if we jump on the couch together?"

She shook her head. "Nah, I just want to read my book.'

"Would you like me to read to you?"

Another head shake. "No, I need to practice my silent reading."

The rejection hurt a little, but I knew it wasn't me. She missed her mom and dad. What little kid wouldn't?

I gave her an adequate amount of space, then busted in the door with silly string and started spraying her in her bed.

She giggled and hid her face in the pillow.

"What's wrong, little girl? Would this help?"

She looked up as I threw her a can of pink silly string. She chased me around the house, then I turned around and chased her around the house. Silly string covered the bathroom, the kitchen, and even the living room. We had silly string in our hair, and I'm pretty sure it stained my couch and the white carpet in my dining room. One or two years ago I would have freaked out due to my OCD, but today I saw it was just silly string. Life was too short not to play so my house could be perfect. It would never be perfect. I knew that now.

We only live once and what was a little scrubbing compared to a sad and confused little girl who wanted her mom? I wasted so much time being serious with Ariel. I was so rigid with rules, I never took time to relax and enjoy the moment I was in. And now she was gone.

WHEN OUR CANS RAN OUT, picking up the silly string became a new game. We picked it all up in about five minutes, and we laughed the whole time, racing to see who could pick up the most string.

After she had a bath and I had a shower, we popped some popcorn and snuggled on the couch to watch a movie. I picked her up off the couch around eight o'clock and carried her to Ariel's bed. She opened her eyes sleepily and looked into my eyes.

"I miss Ariel," she said.

My eyes watered. "Me too." I smiled at her.

"Thank you for being my friend, Maddy." She smiled and closed her eyes.

I sat there rubbing my fingers through her hair. I was going to miss her when Whitney and Josh came home, but I could not keep her forever.

ON MONDAY AFTERNOON, I ran into Brad in the hallway. He glared at me when I approached him. "Hello, Brad."

"It's Principal Jones," he said in a stern voice, unfamiliar to me.

Whitney had mentioned the changes in him, but it wasn't until the kiss with Tim that I finally saw the new Brad for myself.

"What do you want?"

In all the years I'd been with him, I had never seen him act this way. The anger and hate in his eyes shot at me like daggers, and his constant smile was missing. Even when we were going through our divorce, he did not show this much hate. He acted as if a switch was turned off. I tried to ignore it, and be professional.

"I was hoping to rent a dunk tank for the spring carnival, and I was wondering if you might want to sit in it."

He did not even look at me. "No," he said and turned away.

"Principal Jones?" I said, even though it did not feel right, the way it rolled off my tongue.

"You can find someone else. I'm not doing it and that's that," he said.

I stared at his back as he walked away. He turned around and finally looked at me. "And if you ever make out with a staff member in your classroom again, you're fired. Do you understand me?"

I nodded.

He continued walking away. Even his walk was heavy and angry, his chest puffed out, and it was all my fault.

I peeked my head into Whitney's room. Tim was at his desk, his attention on the pen in his hand and a notebook he was scribbling in. I knocked and he looked up and waved me in. At least someone was happy to see me.

I sat down at the table in front of him.

"What's up?"

"Is this a good time? I don't want to bother you if you are busy." I was used to him coming in to see me during lunch or prep time. It just seemed weird after our date and all. Did he think we were a couple?

"Absolutely. It's nice to see you in here for a change." He looked me up and down, a question in his eyes. "Is everything okay?"

I clenched my hands in fists. "It's the principal," I said through clenched teeth.

"Mr. Jones? What happened?"

Concern was written all over his face. "Is this about him

seeing us kiss the other day? You aren't getting fired, are you?"

"No, but he's pretty upset. I've never seen him like this before."

"I'll talk to him," he said. He was trying to be helpful, but talking to Brad would only make things worse. Tim had no idea of the history between Brad and me. I probably should tell him, but I wasn't ready.

"No, please don't. Let me handle this. Promise?"

He shook his head. "Okay, if you think so."

"I really do."

He turned in his chair. "Eh, maybe the guy just needs to get laid."

Was he trying to get a reaction from me? I never wanted to know about Brad's sex life. Then I remembered he knew nothing at all. Or did he?

"Tim, what do you know that you aren't telling me?"

He got up and shut his door. "Listen, I was walking back to my room from the lunchroom and I heard someone in the gym. A couple teachers were talking about some get-together this weekend that by the way I was not invited to, were you?"

I shook my head. I avoided telling him I knew about the party and heard them talking last week. He would probably spot the jealousy in my voice, which would lead to more questions.

"Anyway, the ladies were talking about how Brad was there and he had too much to drink. He told them all he needed to quit being such a pushover and start acting like their boss. Some woman came to pick him up and no one knew who she was. That Mrs. Banks, I think her name is, said she thought the woman was Mr. Jones' girlfriend or new catch or something."

His words hit like bricks against my heart. I blinked away the tears because I could not cover up another running and crying scene. I thought if he hooked up with someone other than Lisa, it wouldn't hurt me, but the pain in my chest was suffocating me. I had to focus on filling my lungs with air.

"Yeah, I don't know," was all I could say.

Tim's phone dinged. He looked at the face then turned it over on his desk.

"Need to get that?"

He shook his head. "Nah. There is one more thing," he said. "Mr. Jones came in here a few minutes ago to tell me he's holding a teachers' meeting after school today in the gym. He said it was mandatory."

Something was definitely going on, and I no longer had a clue what Brad was up to. He was not the man I married. Did I ever really know him at all?

11

I received the email from Brad about the mandatory meeting in the gym after school. I had a hard time focusing the rest of the day, worried about what the meeting could be about. Would he get rid of Tim? Make a scene and get himself into trouble? Have a nervous breakdown in front of everyone? If he was seeing someone, why did he care so much about Tim and me?

Lisa came into the library to retrieve her class and never even looked my way, which was better than some rude remark or her throwing out a 'Miss Jones' just to get to me. I was okay with silence.

I was the first teacher in the gym for the meeting. I pulled up a chair and took out my phone to avoid looking at Brad as he tested out the microphone. Our eyes met from across the room and I smiled, but he looked away without the slightest expression. Who was this man? He had changed so much in just a couple days.

Once the teachers filed in, including Tim who sat to my right, Brad cleared his throat and stepped up to the microphone.

"I'm sure everyone is wondering why I called a last-minute teachers' meeting today. First of all, I want to apologize for any inconvenience. We have a lot of changes to make, and you need to be notified in person starting with teacher interaction."

Tim and I exchanged confused glances.

"It has come to my attention that some teachers may be dating and putting on public displays of affection in this school."

Everyone erupted in loud whispers, and Tim raised an eyebrow. I looked around the room to see if anyone suspected us. They all looked confused so I highly doubted they knew about the incident he was referring to. I was sure that was not information Brad would disclose because I was his ex-wife and that would just be wrong.

"That is not acceptable behavior in this school and if it continues, there will be consequences such as unpaid time off. What you do on your private time does not come into this school. The school atmosphere needs to be more professional. What are we teaching the children? I expect professionalism. Do you all understand?"

More confused looks and loud whispers erupted all around us.

Tim leaned toward me. "I think he's a little bitter. He definitely has the hots for you."

"Stop," I said looking around to make sure no one heard him.

"During your prep time, you are not chatting with other teachers. We have prep time for a reason."

Mrs. Thomas raised her hand. She stood up and started speaking before Brad had a chance to acknowledge her.

"We are a team, and sometimes we like to help each other out by combining projects with other classrooms or whatever that teacher may need help with. If we are busy with our own stuff, obviously we don't, but there are just some things that are better when we team up."

She sat down and a long moment of silence followed while he burned a hole through her with his angry stare. "It sounds to me like you guys don't need a prep time at all."

Lisa stood up while raising her hand. She did not wait for his acknowledgment before she spoke either. "You can't take our prep time away. Teachers need that time. If you do that, you will have a lot of angry teachers at the next schoolboard meeting."

"You're always welcome at a schoolboard meeting. Heck, I prefer it. But if you are all using your time wisely, I won't have to take them away, Miss Banks."

She dropped to her seat, her mouth still open.

Wow. Did that just happen?

Although I was offended since this whole meeting was obviously about me, I took secret pleasure in Brad putting Lisa in her place. Even growing up, she was rich and spoiled. Her parents and teachers always gave her what she wanted. She had a way of manipulating people into thinking she was a good person, but she targeted others. Brad was not having any of it. Even though she had cooked him food and catered to him this past year, she was not getting her way with him and that shocked her. She had no idea how to handle being turned down. Usually, her persistence helped her get what she wanted, but not today.

AN OLDER SECOND GRADE TEACHER, Mrs. Voss, stood up. "I'm not sure who you are suggesting acted this way, but I have never seen anything like that happen in our school. I'm not sure where you got your information from, but I can speak for everyone here that it is a lie. No one would act that way in the school, and the only people who had a relationship in this school are you and Madeline. I'm sorry, I know you two have been through a lot, but this is uncalled for."

She shot me an apologetic look before sitting back down.

I ducked my head, not wanting to hear how he was going to respond. This was escalating fast. and I was not ready for it. I'd heard enough for one day.

"I agree. I know it's hard to believe, but it needed to be addressed. I would not bring it to your attention if it wasn't a concern."

A few teachers stood up to leave, obviously not wanting to hear any more.

"One last thing," he said. He leaned into the microphone and looked me directly in the eye as he said, "There will be no spring carnival this year."

A gi-normous uproar erupted. and everyone started yelling at him.

"You can't do that," I said loud enough for everyone to hear. But he walked off the stage and ignored me.

All the teachers were busy telling each other how unfair he was being. They did not realize he had already walked out.

Brad called the meeting to make everyone as miserable as he was, and it definitely worked. But he was making a terrible mistake. The children and their parents looked forward to the spring carnival all year. We had bouncy houses, games, cotton candy machines, snow cone machines, popcorn, face painting, yard games, and prizes outside, and BINGO in the cafeteria with cupcakes and sprinkles. Parents volunteered and spent the day getting to know the kids' friends. Teachers loved using the spring carnival to keep the kids in line when they had spring fever and struggled to focus or were misbehaving. "You don't want to miss the spring carnival," we'd say. Or, "we need to get this school work done so we can go to the spring carnival."

"I can't believe he left right after throwing that out there. It was a coward move," Mrs. Thomas said.

"Maybe he's having a bad day," Tim said.

Lisa shook her head. "He's not winning this battle without a fight. Who is with me?"

I sat there and listened to everyone while nodding in agreement. I could not help but feel guilty, and I hoped no one would tell me I should talk to him. I wanted to stay out of this. He was no longer my husband.

I snuck out of the gym without telling anyone. I needed to cool down and a walk sounded like the best way. My feet took me into the woods, and I followed the path to the pond.

Brad was there, hunched over, his hands covering his eyes.

I turned around to sneak out before he saw me, a little annoyed that he was in the only place that gave me solace on the worst days. I hoped this would not become a normal hiding place for him.

His phone rang and I jumped behind the nearest tree because it scared the crap out of me.

He stood up and groaned before saying, "Hello."

"How is everything? Is there anything I can do? I hate this. I'll tell her, I promise. I'm just not ready yet. I'm so angry with her right now, and I don't even know if she would listen to me if I tried to tell her. No, you don't need to call her. I'll call you back after school. Love you, too."

He picked up a rock and threw it as far as he could, and then yelled, "Why? Why?!"

He turned around, and for the second time today we locked eyes. Although this time he looked guilty. I turned and followed the trail out of the woods and kept running until I reached the school. I grabbed my keys, and listened to make sure I did not hear any footsteps. Everyone was gone now except the janitor and maybe a teacher or two in the North wing.

Once at my car, I fumbled with my keys. I looked around to make sure he was not trying to find me. That guilty look in his eyes haunted me. Was that the girlfriend he was seeing? Was he planning on telling me about it? Although I would never admit it to anyone, I was devastated.

JOSH SHOWED up around five to pick up Brittany. His eyes were all red and puffy. "They think Whitney has some internal bleeding so they have to run more tests. I'm going to stay in town for a couple more days, and my parents are coming up to hang out with Brittany tomorrow."

Internal bleeding? "Is she going to be okay?"

"Yeah, they're just being careful. I'm not sure what you have going on this weekend, but maybe you could see her."

"I'd love to," I said. "Maybe I'll go up there tonight and take a sick day tomorrow. The school has been, well, chaotic."

"Chaotic?"

"Yeah, have you talked to Brad lately?"

"No, I haven't had a chance."

"He's been a little ... off. Anyway, I'm sure it's nothing."

I did not want to burden Josh and Whitney. They had enough going on, and if Josh told Whitney, she would try to solve the problem like she always did. My best friend was not afraid to get involved. If she had been in the gym today, she would have put Brad in his place.

"I'm sure it isn't easy for him either, with you back in the school. The two of you have a lot of history."

"Yeah, I know. But it's like I don't even know him anymore. Anyway, I'll probably head to the hospital tonight instead and call in tomorrow. The drive may help clear my head. It has been a long day."

"I hear ya," he said. "I'm so excited to sleep in my own bed."

"Hey, Josh, can I ask you a question?"

"Anything," he said.

"Do you know if Brad is seeing anyone?"

"Not that I know of." He took a step closer to me. "Did you hear he is?"

"No, I just ... I don't know what I was thinking. Please don't mention I asked, okay?"

"You have my word."

Brittany came out of Ariel's bedroom, dragging her backpack and suitcase. "Help, please."

I grabbed her blanket and pillow and walked them to their car. I buckled her in and kissed her forehead.

"Thank you, Maddy. I love you," she said.

"I love you, too," I said back. Those words never got old. "Now, you come back and see me soon, okay?"

She nodded.

As I watched them drive away, I became teary eyed. It was so hard to see her go. I never thought I'd become this attached to her so fast. Here I was scared to even have her over. I needed this road trip more than I thought. I needed to see my best friend.

I MADE up a bed on the couch in her hospital room, careful not to wake up Whitney. Bags hung next to her IV drip.

When the nurses came in to take her vitals, she opened her eyes and smiled at me. "You came."

"Of course I came," I said. "I couldn't let you have all this fun alone."

She pulled the sheets over her gown.

"Thank you for skipping school to be with me."

"I won't even be missed. Mrs. Anderson is subbing for me

again so I'm sure the kids will be thrilled. Although I will be sorting book for days because she doesn't know how to put any of them where they belong."

"How are things with the rock-climber guy?"

I laughed. "Good, until Brad caught us kissing, that is. I don't think he is real happy about it even though I'm pretty sure he's seeing someone anyway."

"How do you know that?"

"Teachers were talking, you know. Plus I heard him on the phone about keeping it a secret, and I'm sure he was speaking to a woman."

Whitney's arm twitched and I jumped.

"Sorry, it does that sometimes. All these IV's and stuff. I don't think he's seeing someone else."

"Well, it's not Lisa, that's all I know. She pretty much bit his head off at the teachers' meeting today."

"Teacher's meeting? Hang on a sec, he never had teachers' meetings before."

"Yeah, he said we need to be more professional, no PDA at school, you know."

She started laughing so loud I thought she was going to hurt herself.

"What's so funny?"

"Sounds like he had a meeting because he's not happy about you kissing Tim."

I nodded. "Pretty much. He's changed a lot. I don't even recognize him anymore."

"I'm sure he's just hurt. Can you blame him? He also lost his daughter and spouse, you know."

I grabbed her hand. "No more taking about boring school stuff. When do you get to come home?"

"Well, I won't be back teaching before the end of the school year. I have some other issues the doctors want to investigate and run a million more tests. Then I'll at least be home in time to lay in the sun in our back yard. Maybe I'll come to your house and hang out by the lake."

"You know you're always welcome."

We talked until close to ten, when the nurses told me I needed to let her sleep. I hung out the next day until the doctors began her tests. I hated leaving her there all by herself, but she assured me she was fine.

"Hey Maddy," she said as I was getting ready to leave. "Thank you for all your help with Brittany. Josh and I really appreciate it. I'm sure it wasn't easy, you know, with having Brittany in Ariel's room, and everything."

"To be honest, Brittany has helped me get through so much. I'm finally opening Ariel's bedroom and letting the light in. I should be thanking you."

"I'm glad my injury was such a blessing," she said with a laugh.

I shook my head. "Sassy."

"Would you expect any less?"

He could not erase the picture of that young boy toy and his beautiful Madeline kissing right in the open classroom. The weight in his chest felt unbearable. He wanted to write it off as a mid-life crisis, but she wasn't even forty. She was gorgeous and sweet, and any man would fall for her. There was no one out there like her. He needed to face that he lost the love of his life and his daughter due to his own stupidity. He deserved this.

She was hurt and confused after their daughter passed away on his watch. The guilt consumed him every day. If only he had checked to make sure she was buckled in. Why hadn't he checked? How many times did Madeline tell him Ariel was going to end up hurt if she kept unbuckling?

He never should have let Maddy leave. He thought she would come back. She said she needed some space, and he owed her that much so he moved out. He never expected it would be forever. He had hoped they would end up back together after she had some time to grieve. He knew she blamed him, how could she not? He blamed himself, damn it. Ariel's death was his fault. He lived with that memory every single day. He lost his one and only child and his wife, the love of his life. He hated himself for it. When they met at the attorney's office to sign the divorce papers, he was sure she would not go through with it, but she did, and it broke his heart.

HE SAT down on the bench by the pond, all alone since he scared Maddy away. She could no longer look at him. He tried so hard to talk to her, to let her know he understood, and he was there for her, but she wanted nothing to do with him.

Did she hear him talking on the phone? How was he so stupid not to pay attention and look around? He did not want her to know who he was talking to. Her heart would break if she knew what was going on.

The trees were bare, and the woods never looked so cold and lonely. How could he go on in this world without his two girls? On top of it all, he had to be the principal and her boss, too. She would move on and find a new job soon enough. He was glad she finally started talking to Whitney again. He had talked to Whitney way more than Maddy these last few months. She was worried about Maddy, too.

He did not want to leave the bench and go back to his parent's house. He was a failure, and he hated returning to his childhood home to live with his mommy and daddy. He was too old for that. But if he found his own apartment that would mean he was moving on, and he did not want to move on. Not without his wife. She was his whole world and all he had left.

He stared at the ice-covered water. He remembered the first time Madeline took him on the hidden path in these woods. He was amazed because the wood was right in town. He never expected the hidden pond to be so beautiful. He had no idea back then how much this pond would become a part of his life, his family's life.

The locals who knew about the pond planted flowers and took care of the landscape. On the outside of the woods was another small pond in the shape of the state of Minnesota. Most people never even thought about wandering in the woods where a whole nature scene was hidden. Just coming to the pond gave him a calmness he never felt unless he was there.

He was in shock the first time she showed him what was in the woods. He never would have believed her if he hadn't seen it for himself. The grass was bright green, and the water was so blue. She had taken off her shoes, and he grabbed her hand, begging her to dance with him.

She shook her head at his insane idea, but did not fight him as she put her arm around his neck. He twirled her into the sun, her scarf blowing in the wind. He wanted to stay in that moment forever. He had never done anything like that before, but he was different when he was with her. She helped him to become a better person. The true person he was deep down.

Her beauty was breath taking, and her heart was bigger than he ever thought possible. Their eyes were locked whenever he wasn't twirling her that day, and when he dipped her, her back arched so much he thought she might fall over. He took advantage of one dip and locked his lips on hers as he pulled her back up. She giggled and opened her eyes wide, not letting him stand back up. She'd grabbed his chin and told him she loved him.

Butterflies filled his chest like they had so many years ago when he recalled the night they were pretty sure Ariel was conceived. Skinny dipping in the pond. It was unlike them to be so risky when they could get busted at any minute. They sat on the bench chatting about their lives growing up and their hopes and dreams. He would stop and watch her mouth as she radiated so much passion in her words.

He loved the way her tongue stuck on the roof of her mouth at times, and she would slur a bit. He loved when she put her hand over her eyes every time she was embarrassed. That summer night, as the sun set in the sky, she dared him to jump in the water. He loved the element of surprise, so he figured why not? He took off his clothes and went running into the water. He felt the lily pads and other nasty weeds in the water, but he did not care. He had one goal and that was to get her to jump in after him. He made up some lame excuse about losing his car keys in the water, and she took the bait. She jumped in the pond to help him search for the keys on the mucky bottom. He admitted it was just a scam to get her into the water, and she splashed him when she figured it out.

His first response was to laugh at her, but she surprised him and brought her hands down in the water and slapped him in a place that brought him to tears. They made love right there in the water over the dim light of the moon so high in the sky. That was the day he knew he would marry her, and it only took two months for him to find the perfect moment and the perfect ring. This magical place represented their family, or what their family once was.

It gave him hope that she was still coming down here when she was upset. That meant she had not completely given up on him. Maybe this Tim guy was just a phase, but it still hurt.

The look on Maddy's face when he was full of anger froze him. Didn't she see how much he loved her? Did she really want that child-like man? He could not bear the thought. He wanted his old life back. He could not control the burning flames in his heart that made him say things out of anger, without thinking.

He pulled his grandmother's locket out of his pocket. Before she died, she gave the locket to him and told him to give it to Ariel when she was old enough to take care of it. He had put a photo of his wife on one side and his daughter on the other. When he was having a bad day, he would reach into his pocket and run his thumb over the locket's curves. He missed his family so much.

He needed to fix this, to make things right with Maddy, but how? The image of the day he walked into her room and saw them kissing came back. The smile on her face. When was the last time he saw her smile?

He gave her everything he had in the divorce except what his attorney made him keep. He was back at home with his parents, just a few doors down from her. He would stare up at the moon at night and wonder if she was doing the same. They would never be the same together, but he wanted to try. Would she ever forgive him?

His anger always got the best of him, and now she would never forgive him after canceling the spring carnival. How could he take it back and make it right? He needed to try. That he knew.

She told him to move on, and that she did not care who he dated. Did she know she would always be the only one for him? He would rather die alone than replace the spot next to him in bed with anyone else. If only she felt the same.

He thought putting everything into his job and accepting this principal position would distract him enough to avoid the pain, but his heart was in pieces. She was hurting, and he needed to figure out a way to make it all right again.

13

The school vibe completely changed. I went to lunch in the break room for the first time since I'd returned to work just so I could find out what I had missed. Also because if I was alone with Tim on my lunch break and Brad found out, he was sure to punish the whole school again. Whitney may think it is because he still loved me, but I think his ego was hurt, and he in no way wanted me to move on.

Early as always, I sat down at the far end of the room. As the teachers came through the door, they all raised an eyebrow and said hello to me. Some were more friendly and welcoming than others. Lisa came in and sat down next to me, even though there were many open spots.

Tim sat down on the other side of me. Small conversations were going on, and I was waiting for someone to bring up our principal. I hoped they would not stop talking about him because I was there.

"Tim, you're still here? Do you know when Whitney is coming back?" Mr. Erickson, one of the first-grade teachers said.

Tim pulled in his chair. "I'm not sure, but it sounds like she won't be back until next year." He looked at me. "Right?"

I nodded.

"And what about Principal Jones?" Lisa said out of nowhere, staring directly at me. She was so close I could smell the onions on her breath.

"What about him? You seem to keep better tabs on him than any of us, Lisa."

I heard a few snorts from the other teachers and big eyes as they tried to hold in their surprised reactions.

She let out a squeal after glaring at the teachers who reacted to my comment. "Well, someone has to. You aren't the only one who lost a daughter, Madeline. He is human, too."

Just when I thought she was done, her voice grew louder.

"Why do you think he's going so crazy and being so mean? It's your fault he took the carnival away. We all know you blame him for the accident, but stop punishing him. Grow up. Your marriage failed long ago and you both know that, so quit being such a bitch."

Saying bitch in a cafeteria full of elementary school teachers showed how angry she was about this whole thing. Canceling the school carnival was a serious matter to teachers.

"That's not fair," one of the teachers said.

I looked over and Tim's chin dropped. This was a horrible way for him to find out about Brad. He looked shocked, hurt, and angry.

I cleared my throat. "What exactly do you think I can do?"

She stood up, her chair squealing as she pushed it back. "You could start by talking to him. Tell him not to cancel it."

"You're the one who follows him around and flirts with him every day, you talk to him," I said.

I tossed my lunch in my lunchbox and walked out. Maybe

it wasn't the most professional thing to do, but I held my head high and booked it back to my classroom. That was exactly why I never ate in the break room with the other teachers.

Tim knocked on my door only moments later. I really didn't want to deal with this right now.

"I'm sorry," I said, before he had a chance to say anything.

"Why didn't you tell me?"

I leaned my head into my hand. "It never came up." I walked over to him. "My relationship with Brad is over. Yes, were married and—"

"Oh, Braaaad," he said. "I guess you didn't lie. You told me it was Brad you were married to. I just didn't put two and two together."

"Are you mad?"

"How can I be mad? It's in your past. It's just … so much makes sense now."

My phone rang and distracted us.

I picked it up. "It's Whitney."

"Go ahead," he said backing away.

"You sure? I don't want our conversation to end this way."

He smiled. "I think I'm finally rubbing off on you. You like me. You care if I'm mad at you."

I laughed. "Get out of here." I waved him off and answered the phone.

He winked and shut my door.

"Are you lost yet without me?" she said.

I couldn't help but laugh. "You have no idea. How are you? How did the surgery go?"

"I'm being discharged tomorrow so I should be home sometime in the afternoon. I was hoping you'd come over and we can have a movie marathon of *Scream* while we lay in bed all day and pig out on junk food like teenagers. If you don't have plans, that is."

"I don't know. I'm a pretty busy lady. What will Brittany and your husband think about that?"

"They're going to see his sister up north, and I thought we could have a girls' night and sleepover?" she said, her voice high and hopeful.

"I may have to check my busy schedule," I said. "But seriously, I can't wait. Work has been a big mess. You won't believe it when I tell you."

"I feel like I've missed so much. You'll have to tell me everything. By the way, I don't know how things went with Brittany, but she can't stop talking about you. I better be careful or she's going to leave me for you."

I laughed. "We had a really good time. She was exactly what I needed, I'm so glad Josh called. I needed a little push, and I'm so glad I got to spend some time with her."

"Me too. Well, I'd better go. Thanks again for taking Britt all those days. Time to get my vitals checked. I swear these nurses never leave my room. See you tomorrow."

I ran into Brad on my way out the door. We were walking toward each other, and I was trying to build up the nerve to say hello, but he turned into the office in front of me. I just kept walking.

I TOOK off my heels and flopped down on my couch to snuggle up with my favorite afghan. I could see the cloudy sky from the bay window, and the air was so chilly and muddy this time of year. I turned onto my side, the picture on the end table next to my couch catching my eye. Our last professional photo as a family, just six months before the accident. I had pulled out a few pictures last night and hung them up because I was done hiding from them. I picked up the photo and hugged it close to my chest. So many memories circled in my head. I studied her face, her sweet hands, her smile that was so big it showed her missing tooth. The little scar above her right eye from when she fell on her bicycle and hit the handlebars.

She would never get to graduate from high school or even from elementary school. She would never have the chance to chase boys and get married. She would never know what it feels like to have her first kiss or to have children. She was way too young to die. Why her?

Ariel had her arms around Brad and my shoulders in the photo. We all had big grins because the photographer was making us laugh. We were so happy back then.

The smile on Brad's face was so real, so bright. A frown now replaced that smile, and dark circles highlighted his gentle eyes.

I set the photo down because it hurt too much to remember.

"How are you feeling?"

Whitney fluffed up the pillow on her lap and handed it to me to put behind her back. "I'd be much better if I could walk."

"I bet it's hard because you're so active. I would love a chance to sit home and sleep all day."

"It seems more exciting than it is. I'm just glad to be home."

"I bet. No one wants to be stuck in a hospital bed."

"I'd rather talk about you. Let's spend the night watching movies and having girl time. I'm sick of feeling depressed. Now tell me about Tim. Is he a better teacher than I am?"

I laughed. That was the Whitney I knew. "No. He does a good job though. The kids love him."

"I bet he's a better kisser than I am."

I gasped. "Really? You just had to go there, didn't you? For your information, I wouldn't know. I've never kissed you."

"Well, I'm married, but I think my husband would approve as long as he could watch."

I nodded my head. "That sounds about right."

"Sounds like you and Britt had a good time. You doing okay?"

"She's a little ray of sunshine. She got me to open up Ariel's room and at first it was tough, but it should be open. Her room was becoming a dark place, and that isn't right. We sure played a lot of Barbies. That girl has quite the imagination."

"Yes, she does. And Brad?"

What could I say about Brad? "What about Brad? I don't really have anything to say except he has been a total jerk, and I avoid him at all cost."

"You know how I feel about that. It's because he's jealous."

"I don't know."

"Well, I have something that will make you feel better."

She pulled a pink envelope out from under her pillow.

"After everything you've been through, you're still thinking of me. You didn't need to do this."

"Just open it."

I grabbed it and shook my head as I carefully opened the envelope.

"Great idea, by the way, the way you had someone else write the last letter for me."

"I had to get it to you somehow. I thought it was cute."

"It was more surprising than cute."

"Just open it," she said nodding at the envelope I held in my hand.

14

A t three o'clock on a Monday afternoon, all the teachers were sitting in the cafeteria, staring at him. He knew they expected the worst. How could he blame them? He had once again kept them after school. He tested out the microphone, and his gaze instantly found Madeline. She was sitting in the back row as if she would rather be anywhere but here. Could he blame her? She hardly even glanced his way as he started to speak.

"I am deeply sorry for making you stay after school for the second time in a week. I know you all have families you want to go home to and things to do. I want to apologize for how the meeting went last week."

Their mouths opened into giant o's, and quiet whispering erupted throughout the room. He cleared his throat. He was never one to be at a loss for words, but he had to dig deep.

"I canceled the spring carnival without speaking with all of you first. I was being impulsive and wrong and I want to apologize. I wasn't considering all of you when I did what I did, and I had absolutely no right to make that decision based on impulse. We are a team here, and I have not been a great leader lately." He paused to smile and hoped it showed his sincerity. "As many of you know, I lost my daughter less than a year ago. My grief has interfered with my job, and I'm sorry."

He looked at Madeline, and held his breath as she got up and left the room. His heartfelt apology came to an abrupt end as he said the words that broke his heart. "I have decided to take a leave of absence while I get my mind right. Maybe even step down as principal."

"No, you can't, we need you," Lisa said.

"We all make mistakes," Mr. Erickson said.

Everyone was loudly chatting amongst themselves, and he figured it was a good time to leave. He chased Madeline down the hallway. He should let her be, but he couldn't, not yet. He knew he owed her an apology.

"Madeline, Madeline, Maddy!" He moved fast to catch her. Her face was pale, and red blotches broke out around her eyes.

She pushed him away, but he caught his balance and placed his hands on her shoulders. "I'm sorry. I probably shouldn't have mentioned it, but I had to tell them why I've been acting so out of line. They're like family, and I owe it to them. I canceled the spring carnival because I was angry at you. That kiss was so hard for me to see, can't you understand that?"

"It's always about you, Brad. I know you blame me for what happened to Ariel. You don't think I can see how looking at me makes you cringe?"

He shook his head. How could she blame herself? She wasn't even in the damn car. The accident was his fault. He should have buckled her in, and he never should have stopped on the side of the road.

"What do you mean? It's my fault, we both know it's my fault. Why would you say that?"

She covered her face with her hands. "I wanted it to be your fault, I did, but all along I knew it was my fault. I should have been there with you guys. It's all my fault." She dropped her hands and snuck past him.

He was in too much shock to stop her. She was not thinking clearly. "There is something you need to know about that day." He ran his hand through his hair, trying to find the words, and then he saw him. Tim. He headed over to Tim, pulled his fist back, and suddenly found himself on the floor unable to breathe. What just happened?

Tim crouched down, holding out his hand. "You okay?"

Brad slapped Tim's hand away and stood up. His head throbbed. He ran his hand over his head and found a goose egg forming on the back of his head.

"That was quite a fall." Tim put his hand on Brad's shoulder and squeezed a little too tight.

He was too unsteady to push Tim's hand off.

"Wow," Madeline said. She shook her head at them and went into her classroom. "Grow up, Brad."

HE TOOK the rest of the day off because if he saw Tim, who knew what he would do. He should not trust his own instincts right now. His heart was broken and was acting off impulse lately.

He had been staring at his phone all day, waiting for it to ring. All these damn visitor restrictions made it impossible for him to make his way into the ICU to see his father. The worst of the pandemic was hopefully over and the world was starting to go back to normal, but he couldn't help but wonder if masks would forever be the new policy in hospitals.

He picked up his phone, and she answered it on the first ring. "Lyndsey, it's me. Did you find any way to get me in?"

"No, it's terrible. Security is horrible. They only let two people in per patient each day. Did you get my message? We're still waiting for the doctor to come in and tell us how it went. This is just so scary. I need you here."

He was so angry about everything at work, he forgot to check his phone.

"I don't care what it takes, I'm going up there. What room is it again?"

"Three forty-three. If you can reach the elevator, just push third floor and it's the first left out of the elevator, first door on your right. You can't miss it. Are you sure this is a good idea?"

"What are they going to do? Arrest me?"

He hung up and pulled the mask out of his other pocket and secured it behind his ears.

THE ELECTRONIC DOORS opened as he neared the entryway. An elderly woman with gray hair stood behind a table. He could not tell if she was smiling because the mask took up half her face.

"Hello, sir. What are you here for today?"

He planned on saying he was there for an appointment, but he did not go to this clinic, and he could not remember one doctor's name for the life of him. He needed to think fast. "I'm here to pick up a prescription."

"Okay, do you have any Covid symptoms? Shortness of breath, a fever, a new cough?"

He shook his head. He felt so guilty for lying. He did not like to be dishonest, but the situation was desperate.

She handed him a sticker with Tuesday typed in green letters.

"Put this on your shirt and go ahead."

"Thank you."

His hands shook as he placed the sticker on his shirt. He made his way to the pharmacy. He glanced back at the woman. She was talking to another woman and her young daughter. Definitely not watching him at all. He walked past the pharmacy and into the long hallway. His shoulders tightened at the thought that someone would come running after him and tell him he needed to leave. He looked back again, but no one seemed to care.

He passed a woman in scrubs and a medical mask in the hallway. She said hello and he nodded and smiled, but no one could see his smile under the mask. Although right now he was thankful, because his nerves would probably give him away.

He found his way to the elevator and pushed three. As the doors closed, he let the air out of his lungs and wiped the sweat from his brow. He made his way into the room, and his mom and sister's faces lit up

"I'm so sorry, we are not a dishonest family," his mom told the nurse in the room.

"Don't apologize. If I were in your shoes I would do the same thing."

He wrapped his arms around Lyndsey, her shoulders and head collapsed against him in sobs. "It's so bad, Brad. It's just so bad."

"What's going on?" he said to anyone who would answer.

"I'm sorry, we didn't want to tell you until we talked to the doctors," his mom said. She sat down on the empty hospital bed and looked out the window.

"Mom, what is it? What happened? He went in for knee surgery and ended up in a second emergency surgery? What the hell is going on?" He couldn't help the panic in his voice now that he was here and could see his father lying so helpless in the hospital bed.

His mother grabbed his hand, and he relaxed a bit.

"He had an obstruction in his colon, and he went into septic shock. We don't know what is happening now."

The nurse peeked her head into the room. "The doctor is on his way now." She looked at Brad. "You may want to go down the hall and get a coffee, just in case."

"No problem. Thank you for letting us know," his mother said.

"I have to be honest, if it was my dad I would do the same," the nurse said.

Her response surprised him.

"We don't have any rules here in the ICU," she said.

"Why don't the two of you get some coffee. I don't think it's a good idea if we are all here when the doctors come in," his mother said with tears in her eyes.

He hated to leave her, but she was right.

"Why don't two of you stay? It's better if there are two of the patient's family to remember what the doctors say," the nurse said.

Lyndsey nodded.

He made his way down the hall. The coffee machine had black coffee, but no cups.

He scrolled through his phone to waste time, but social media was so depressing. Everyone made their lives seem so perfect. He looked up Madeline. She hadn't posted anything for months. Her page had a bunch of condolence comments after their daughter's death. He switched off his phone. No way was he going to read those. He stared out the window, hands on his hips for what felt like hours.

A tap on his shoulder startled him. He turned around to find Lyndsey in tears.

"What is it? What did they say?"

"He was in sepsis, septic shock."

"What? How? He was just fine yesterday, walking around, right?"

"Yeah. Mom said he was constipated, but fine. He was even walking around non-stop after his knee surgery."

How could he have been so caught up in jealousy and selfishness that he had not called his father after surgery to check on him?

"What else did they say? Is he going to be okay?"

"They had to cut him open and remove some of his intestines after they flushed out the obstruction. They have to keep him sedated and perform another surgery tomorrow."

"Another surgery? For what?" First his daughter and now his father? Would he live through this?

"When they cut his abdomen open, they couldn't stitch him back up because they had to flush out the obstruction. They need to do another surgery to put in a colostomy bag, which they think he may only have for six months or so. They're hoping to stitch him up a little bit more."

"So you're telling me he's lying on the bed with his abdomen wide open?"

She placed her hand on his shoulder to steady him. The tears swelled up in the back of his eyes, but he did not want Lyndsey to see him cry. He needed to be strong for her and his mother.

"No, no. He has a wound vac to seal it, and he's covered with a blanket and gauze."

He pulled away from her. "I have to see him." He hurried down the hall and into the room next door.

"Wait, Brad!"

HIS MOTHER WAS STARING at his father, holding his hand. Brad wiped the tears running down her face and held her. "Everything is going to be okay, mom. Dad is a fighter."

Then he saw the tube coming out of his father's mouth, and his tongue hanging out.

"Dad?" His voice sounded unfamiliar. "Is that a breathing tube?" He looked back at his sister who was entering the room.

"You didn't let me finish."

He closed his eyes, hoping it would all disappear when he opened them up. This was a nightmare he could not wake up from. Memories of the way his baby girl looked when the paramedics put her in the back of the ambulance came rushing back. She was unconscious after the crash. He screamed her name, but he knew she wouldn't answer. He knew she was already gone. As the ambulance got ready to shut the doors with her in it, he jumped in the back. He waited for the sirens to turn on as it drove away, but the sirens never turned on, and the ambulance driver seemed to be in no hurry.

"How are you doing, ma?" He touched her arm, and she grabbed his hand and held it in place.

"His kidneys are failing, and they said he's too critical to move right now. They're giving him medication to help flush his kidneys, but who knows if that will work. They said he needs to be on dialysis but they don't have the capability here, and they think he's too critical to be moved."

"Don't give up, mom. We're here to help you as a family."

His mother nodded at him. He gave her arm a warm squeeze then locked himself in the bathroom to breathe. He had to show he was strong for her but deep inside he was crumbling.

15

I was glad Brad did not show up at school the next day. His behavior was out of line, and I worried what he would do next. His absence assured me he would be unable to pull another after-school meeting. He was too unpredictable these days. He tried to hit another teacher in the school. That was so unlike him, and then for Tim to react so quickly and lay him flat out like that. It almost felt like it happened in slow motion.

I felt a bit bad for him. I had been hard on him, and I hurt him with Tim. He was suffering some emotional instability. We dealt with our grief in different ways, but yet I still expected him to react like I did.

Ariel was still the first thing I thought about each morning, but going past her door on my way to the kitchen felt a little less suffocating than it used to. I no longer kept her door shut, thanks to Brittany.

I was sure having her around would make me anxious, and I assumed keeping up with her would be difficult considering my lack of energy, but she had cheered me right up. I hated that she would no longer be staying with me. It gave me a good reason to get up each morning. I had someone relying on me. Having her stay with me was a blessing.

My phone lit up across my bedroom. I ran for it, Lyndsey popped up on my screen. Lyndsey?

I had not heard from Brad's sister since the divorce. She likely avoided me because she did not know what to say or where she fit in after I was no longer her brother's wife. Why is it people think they need to take sides after two people split up? Lyndsey was one of my best friends. We hung out all the time when I was married to Brad. When Ariel passed away, she came over every day to hang out, cook dinner, and to listen for the first few days. I tried to get rid of her because I was so depressed I wanted to shut the world out, but she would not let me. Then when Brad and I spit shortly after, she stopped coming. Her texts got shorter and shorter. I had no hard feelings. I knew she felt torn. Brad was her brother, after all. I stopped talking to her too, and my texts got shorter and shorter, and I didn't always answer the door for her. Maybe it was more mutual than I thought.

I tried not to act surprised when I picked up the phone. "Hey, Lyndsey. What's going on?"

I heard the heavy sobs. "It's my dad, he went in for surgery and ended up in septic shock. It's not good. His kidneys are failing."

My jaw dropped, but I stayed silent while she filled me in on all the details. Once she was done, her deep sobs resumed.

"I'm so sorry. How are you? Is there anything I can do?"

She paused again, sniffling a bit. "Could you talk to Brad? I know the two of you aren't together anymore, but you were married for so many years. Please talk to him, he isn't doing well. I'm pretty sure he went down to the pond in the woods. That's where he always goes to process information since ..."

"He never said anything. I had no idea," I said. I had no

idea he was going through so much. No wonder he was so angry. "But I don't think I can right now. We had some words, and the last time I saw him he actually got into a fight with another teacher."

"I didn't know. That doesn't sound like Brad at all. Well, maybe you could sneak up here? I really need a shower, and my mom can't be alone. Dad is still sedated, and they don't plan on waking him up until after the next surgery in the morning. I know it's a lot to ask, and I wouldn't ask if I didn't have to."

"I know. Are the hospitals still requiring masks? I know the pandemic has dwindled—"

"That's the problem, you may have to sneak in."

"Sneak in? Why?" I was a terrible liar. I could not sneak in. "There has to be another way."

"Brad went in through the clinic entrance. They only let two people in a day in the ICU, which is me and my mom. It's the only way."

"What's the room number? I'll be there."

I SPENT the next hour calling every connection I had. The calls were emotionally exhausting. Every time I called someone, they asked me how I was doing because I had not talked to them since the funeral. After calling all the people I knew who worked at the hospital, they all said the same thing and I lost hope. I could not get in the hospital if I wasn't one of the two people visiting the patient. It didn't matter who you knew or what was going on, the rules were strict for a reason, and I had an idea of a way to get it. It went against every moral I had, but I needed to be there for Brad's family, and I had to see my father-in-law because this may be my last chance. This was serious and they were family.

· · ·

I PARKED my car in front of the hospital and stared at the woods. I wanted to run to my happy place down the hill and hide by the pond where it was safe. Instead, I put on my mask before opening up the hospital door. Inside, a man was sitting at a table. He got up and walked over me.

"What are you here for?" he said with empty eyes.

"I'm here to see my dad in room 312."

"Do you have shortness of breath? A recent headache ..." He went on and on, and I kept shaking my head. The fire stirred in my gut, and my face grew hot behind my mask. I did not want to lie, but the truth would get me nowhere near his door.

"Are you one of the two approved visitors?"

"Yes." My mask could not give away the look on my lying face.

He handed me a sticker and led me to another table by the doorway. "Sign in."

I wrote down the room as illegible as I could and signed with just a scribble, making sure they could not make out one letter on the carbon copy beneath. He handed me a clip with 312 laminated on it, and I hung it from my waistband.

I walked through the automatic doors. I heard the man talking to someone else, and I sped up. Would he figure it out? Would I be taking a person away from their loved one in room 312? I walked a little faster.

The hospital had been remodeled since the last time I was there. The elevators weren't where I expected them to be which added to my already anxious mind. I followed a sign for the elevators, but ducked into a bathroom to take a quick break and calm myself. After splashing some water on my face and texting Lyndsey for directions to the room, I opened the door and made my way to the elevator. When the doors opened, I expected someone in it to call me out and make me leave like a child not following the rules, but it was empty.

The doors opened on the third floor, and I made my way down the hall. The door was open just a couple inches and kiddy corner from the nurses station. I did not look directly at the nurses, and kept my head down as I slipped in the door to his room.

I opened the door slowly. "Hello?"

A nurse typing on a computer looked at me, then back at her computer. Lyndsey and Brad's mom, Sue, welcomed me with tears and a tight hug.

"I can't believe you came. Bill will be so happy to know you're here. Although he doesn't look like it, the nurses said he can hear us." She turned back to her strong husband lying helpless on the hospital bed.

Seeing him brought back memories of seeing Ariel's body that day. So cold to the touch. I blinked away the tears.

"Look who's here, Bill, it's Madeline. Madeline is here." She turned back to me. "We've both missed you so much, dear. How did you get in?"

"I don't want to talk about it," I said with a laugh. "I'm a fraud."

"Did you come in the clinic like Brad?"

"No."

She stepped closer to her husband's side and placed her hand over his. "His hands are so cold. Are they supposed to be this cold, Lynds?"

"Maybe we need to cover them up with the blanket."

"Are there any changes with his kidneys?"

"We don't know yet. We're still waiting for the doctor to talk to us."

"Is there anything I can do to help?"

Sue put her hand in mine. "You being here helps."

The nurse checked on the cooler under his bed.

Lyndsey leaned close to me, also watching the nurse fiddle with the cooler. "That's for his knee. The cooler is filled with ice and pushes the cold through the tube and around his knee to help with the swelling. It's pretty cool. The nurse said we get to take it home."

She leaned in again. "Could you hang out for a little while? I want to take my mom home so she can shower maybe even eat something."

"Of course," I said. I was in no rush to return to my empty house.

Lyndsey convinced her mother to go home. "Maddy will call us if anything changes." She glanced at me. "Won't you, Maddy?"

I nodded.

Sue gave me another hug and pushed my hair back behind my ear. "It's so good to see you. I think about you all the time."

I smiled.

The look on Sue's face as she left was complete fear. She did not want to leave him, and who could blame her?

"Hey there, Bill," I said, once they were gone.

I pulled the metal chair next to the bed and held his hand. "I guess I should have come to visit you after, you know, Ariel's accident. I really hope you don't blame me. I should have been in the car with them instead of staying at home trying to make the party perfect with too many decorations. I never got a chance to talk to you, but now seems like a good time. Let's just state the obvious, you really have no choice but to listen to me so sorry about that." I let out a snort, laughing at my own joke.

I wanted his hand to squeeze mine so I knew he heard me. Talking to someone who could not respond was a bit awkward, but I needed to do this. Would he even remember what I was saying when he woke up? I hated to think he might not wake up again. I needed to do this, or I would regret what wasn't said.

Bill was always cracking jokes, which always made me feel more comfortable especially when I first started dating Brad. After my husband proposed to me, Bill took me aside and told me Brad was a lucky man. He told me he could tell I had a true heart, and I never forgot his words.

We went to a karaoke to celebrate the engagement. Bill got up on stage with me, and we sang *I Got You Babe* after six shots of tequila. That was the one and only time I ever saw him drunk, and he was such a hoot. He and Sue danced the night away, he in his cowboy boots and her in her floral dress. I had let too much time pass without seeing them. That was on me.

"The truth is I don't blame Brad for what happened. I wanted to blame him at first but we both know he would do anything he could to protect her. I think the truth is she would still be here today if I had gone with them. I was so caught up in the materialistic nature of a birthday party, I didn't realize that the most important thing was to be with them." I paused and took a deep breath. "Ariel didn't want me to stay home and make everything perfect, she wanted me to go with them but I told her I was too busy. Too busy on her birthday for her? What's wrong with me? I have so many regrets about myself as a mother. And now she's gone forever, Bill. I don't have the chance to make it right because she is gone, and I can't be with Brad because it feels wrong without Ariel. Does that even make sense?"

I wiped away the tears pooling under my eyes. "You have been like a father to me over the years. You know I lost my dad at such a young age. I guess I ran because I couldn't let myself be happy. My body is numb, and it's so hard to feel. I left Brad because I didn't want to stay with him without Ariel. I don't deserve love. Maybe this makes no sense to you, but I don't know if I'll ever have the chance to open up to you like this again.

"The reason I'm telling you all this is because I need you to fight. Fight for Sue and Lyndsey, fight for Brad. Your son lost his only child, and it would kill him to lose you, too. I'm worried about him. He needs you. Please fight. I love him, and I know how much you mean to him, to all of us."

I heard a phone ring behind me, and when I turned around Lyndsay was standing in the doorway. A deer in headlights look crossed her face. How long had she been standing there? How much did she hear?

I dropped Bill's hand and gathered my purse and water bottle off the counter.

"I had no idea," she said as she moved closer to me. "You still love him don't you?"

"Who?" How was I going to cover up my words? I did not even know what they meant. They just came flowing out. I was in no way honest with myself, and I needed time to let my own words sink in.

"Oh, come on, you know who. You need to tell him."

"Tell him what?"

"Tell him you love him. You deserve to be happy and so does he."

I looked away. The glaze across my eyes made it hard to see. I blinked until they cleared again.

She moved closer. "Maddy."

"Please, Lyndsey. Please don't tell him, okay? Just let me process this."

She stared at me for a long moment before she finally answered. "It's really not my place, but he needs you, and you need him. If there is something still there, tell him. I promise I won't say anything, but you need to tell him. You deserve happiness. What the two of you have been through is horrible, but you love each other."

. . .

I STOOD up and hugged her. I looked deep into her eyes. "I promise I will think about it. Thank you for calling me and letting me be here. It really means a lot to me."

She nodded. "You'll always be a part of our family."

I turned around once I reached the door. "Thank you for giving me time to think and not saying anything. I've always thought of you as a sister."

She smiled and let out a loud sob. I walked out the door and down the hall to the elevator. As the doors shut behind me, I cried into my mask.

16

Brad found his sister all alone in the hospital room.

"How are you doing Lynds? Any changes?"

"They said his kidneys are functioning on their own now. He's fighting. I know he is."

He nodded and stood beside her as they both stared at him. A respirator sticking out of his mouth pumped his lungs with oxygen. The machine that fueled the air pulsated, pushing air inside in rhythm.

Another tube was in his nose. Bile from his father's stomach rode up the tube and down again with each breath, making his stomach queasy with every breath his father took.

"Do you remember when we were little and dad would take you hunting, and I'd get to stay home with mom, baking cookies and sleeping on dad's side of the bed.

He nodded.

"She would sing and we would go shopping, and she would tell me not to tell dad. You know how he was about money."

"Yeah, stingy bastard," he said with a laugh.

She laughed along with him. "You know, she used to take me to the gun section and explain which ones dad had or which ones he wanted. I think looking at the guns when she was missing him made her feel a lot less lonely."

"I had no idea she even knew the difference between dad's guns."

"Oh, she knows. I always wanted to go deer hunting with you guys, but girls were never allowed at the shack, and I was always too afraid to ask."

"I didn't know that. I'm sorry, Lynz. Why don't you hunt now?"

She shrugged her shoulders. "I don't know. November gets a little busy, and you two seem to have your routine, and I know it's time for just you and Dad. I don't want to get in the way of that."

"You would never get in the way. We could always skip the shack and stay somewhere else. The guys out there are kind of jerks anyway. You know how dad always goes on about them." He turned and looked her in the eye. "He will get better, Lynds. You said it yourself, he's fighting. He will get through this, I know it."

Lyndsey cleared her throat. "You just missed Maddy, she came up here to visit dad."

He choked on his own air. "Up here? Maddy? How?"

"You aren't the only one who can sneak up here, you know."

"I'm just surprised. She's so straight-laced, not really a rule breaker. And she hasn't been in touch with our family since, you know."

"The two of you have been through something no parent should ever have to go through. You're both hurting, but she loves dad. They had a bond I was a little jealous of, to be honest. She was holding his hand when I walked in after dropping Mom off at home for some food and a nap."

"I'm so glad she came."

"Are you really surprised? She's still the same Maddy deep down, you know. Like you, she's just been through a lot."

He knew she was spot on.

"Is it true you got into a fight with another teacher? Please tell."

"There is nothing to tell. It wasn't a big deal."

"But I heard—"

"Drop it," he said with a deep tone. "And you better not say a word to Mom about it."

"Speaking of Mom, Mr. Crabby pants, will you check on her and maybe bring her back here if she's awake?"

He loved how she always had a way of lightening the mood.

He nodded. "Did Maddy happen to say anything about me?"

Lyndsey seemed to be giving his question careful thought before she answered him. "You know what, don't tell me. I'm sure it's nothing good. We aren't exactly on talking terms. It's been a rough week as you've obviously already heard."

She put her hand on his shoulder and gave it a gentle squeeze.

"All I heard was that you got into a fight with another teacher and she was worried about you. I have a feeling she will come around. You just need to talk to her. Believe it or not, she's worried about you, too."

He avoided telling her he made everything worse every time he opened his big mouth around Maddy. Nor did he want to upset his sister by telling her Maddy had met someone else, and he caught them kissing and that was why he got into a fight with a teacher. He did not want his family taking sides or being angry with her for moving on. She was probably better off without him anyway. Even if he did imagine his fist making contact with the pretty boy's face. He might have missed, and Tim was quicker the last time. He would give him that, but next time he would be faster.

MOST OF THE snow had melted and winter was finally leaving. In its place was mud and brown grass. Spring was truly a magical time in northern Minnesota. The weather could be cold and snow, or warm and sunshine, and changed daily.

Brad's shoes made imprints on the path inside the forest. He stood before the pond and closed his eyes and breathed in the cool spring air. Although all he smelled was dampness and maybe mildew, he felt an overwhelming sense of peace inside the forest. The beauty was unknown to the outside world.

He imagined Ariel running around picking blossoming flowers when summer finally arrived. He taught her to skip rocks a couple years back, and they lay on a blanket, the three of them, and had a picnic in the grass at least once a week. He loved summers because they were out of school and had three months to enjoy the outdoors together.

One time they had a picnic and they were all enjoying sandwiches and Maddy was reading Ariel's favorite Disney princess book full of short stories. He took a big bite of his ham and cheese sandwich on Ezekiel bread, savoring every bite while he listened to his wife's beautiful voice. All of a sudden, damn pigeons came flying around and crapped right on his bread. He was so angry. He dropped the sandwich and chased them around like a crazy person. He was so hangry instantly.

Ariel and Maddy watched him and laughed. Their giggles made him stop being so angry, leaving him laughing with them in the end.

"What, I'm hungry, okay?" he had said.

Big belly giggles escaped from Ariel's sweet little mouth when he finally caught her in his arms.

He set her down.

"He pooped on your bread," Ariel said, pointing at him.

Brad tackled her and tickled her until her face was bright red. Maddy tried to run away, knowing she was next, but he grabbed her arm and pulled her to the blanket, tickling her, too. They were so exhausted from laughing, they lay on their backs to catch their breath. He laughed so hard he felt like he had just done a hundred push-ups.

He turned his head to stare at his beautiful wife, Ariel's head on his belly. She stared back at him with her perfect smile, so filled with love. He grabbed her hand and squeezed it. He was unsure how long they lay there that day, staring at the clouds, but it was a time he would never forget. He never knew their time together would be so short-lived. He thought they had all the time in the world together. Nothing could get between them, or so he believed at the time.

A BIRD SANG BEHIND HIM, bringing him back to the present time. He turned to watch it fly around him. Nature was beautiful and so unpredictable. The bird flew around, and he watched it until it was out of sight. "My sweet Ariel, this world just isn't the same without you."

THE DAYS WERE GETTING LONGER, the sun shining a little later in the day. This small thing gave everyone hope that summer was near. Brad slowed down as he passed the house their family once shared. Maddy's car was in the driveway. He scanned the yard to see if she was outside, but she was nowhere to be seen. He turned into his mother's driveway. He missed driving to work with his wife in the seat next to him. The three of them always went to school together. He missed it.

His head hung as he opened up his screen door and put the key in the door.

"Brad."

Was he imagining her voice in his head? He turned his head slowly. "Maddy?"

She forced a smile.

"What are you ... doing here?"

"I wanted to see how you're doing. I heard about your dad, and I just had to see him. I hope that's okay. I really should have talked to you first but after our fight, I--"

"It's okay, really. No need to apologize." This was the first time she looked at him with kindness, and maybe a little worry in her eyes.

He felt frozen in time, and unsure of how to respond to her. The tenderness had been missing in her eyes for so long. He was in shock to finally see it again. He opened his door.

"Please come in. I'm glad you are here."

"Well, I actually need to get back, I just wanted to tell you in person I'm sorry about your dad."

"Come in. I won't bite, I promise."

She bit her lip.

It tore out a piece of his heart to see her looking so ready to get away.

She surprised him by nodding her head and walking toward him. He stood to the side of the door so he could hold it open for her. She was carrying a casserole pan.

"I made you guys some lasagna. I'm not sure how I can help and I know that ... well ... it helped when people brought me food."

"You hardly ate, remember. We had to throw out all the food people brought. Neither of us felt like eating."

"Well, it was just nice to put it in the oven and smell it cooking, even if we didn't have much of an appetite."

He laughed louder than he expected at the memory, and she gaped. "What's so funny?"

"Nothing."

She took a step toward him, her arms crossed. "I know why you're laughing, and it's not funny."

"It's a little funny. I mean, not at the time, but--"

"It definitely wasn't funny. I can't believe you actually called the fire department."

He grinned. "We had a fire in our oven, Madds."

"I had it under control," she said, her face lighting up as she smiled..

"Sure you did. It took us two days to clean the smoke out of the kitchen and everything it covered."

"It was horrible, but I think it took our minds off everything for a little bit. Sorry I screamed at you that day."

"You were stressed out and grieving. I didn't hold it against you, even if you did start my Vikings shirt on fire."

"It was on the floor. I was using it to try to put out the fire. You would have done the same thing." She looked away, then back. "And I said I was sorry."

"I'm just teasing you."

"I know," she said with a smile and an eye roll.

He was flirting with her, but she seemed to be flirting back. Maybe? Maybe not, but whatever this was, it was definitely a step in the right direction. She looked down as a moment of uncomfortable silence sank in. He tried to think of what to say next or she would make up some excuse to leave. He wasn't ready to let her go yet.

"The doctor said he doesn't think my dad is going to need dialysis anymore. The stuff they gave him seems to be working."

She lifted her head, and her eyes met his. "Oh, that's great news, Brad."

"He's still sedated and he's still on a ventilator, but they're no longer taking it second by second. The doctor said take it minute by minute now. I'm not sure what that means, but it sounds better, right?"

She nodded.

"Yeah. I honestly didn't think my dad was going to make it when his kidneys were failing, and they couldn't move him to a hospital with dialysis."

"Me too."

He held up a can of La Croix. "Want a sparkling water?"

"No, thanks." She took a step toward the door. "I should get home. I made lasagna for myself, and it's in the oven right now. I don't want to start another fire," she said with a wink.

He laughed along with her. "I love seeing you smile." He instantly regretted saying it out loud.

"See you later?"

A question more than a statement? He nodded.

"Tell your mom if she needs anything to please let me know."

He nodded again.

"Also, if you need anything I'm just a couple doors down. Please don't be afraid to ask."

He wanted to take her up on that so badly and tell her he just wanted her to stay, but she would never say yes to that.

"Thanks, Maddy. For the lasagna."

She shut the door behind her, and he watched her walk away through the window. She was so beautiful. He remembered the way her hair felt when he ran his fingers through it. The way she smelled when she snuggled up next to him on the couch at night as they watched *The Notebook* over and over again. It was her favorite movie and he liked the way she always snuggled up next to him when they watched it, as if for the first time. He even missed the way she used to keep him up at night snoring in his arms, but he could not bear to wake her and risk disturbing her sleep. He loved everything about her, even on the days they fought. A part of him wished he didn't. It would not hurt this bad.

17

I waited until I was out of his sight before I wiped my tears. I had to cross my arms to stop them from touching him. I hated that I was still in love with him. I did not want to love him anymore. We could not be a family without Ariel. We could not be happy without her. Going on with life as though she never existed felt wrong. What kind of mother would I be?

I walked and walked until I found myself at the bridge. The traffic was light this time of day.

The lake was no longer covered in a layer of ice, but the water was still cold. About as dark and cold as my heart since I lost Ariel.

I TOOK out my phone and made a call to the one person who always made me feel better.

"Hello," she said.

"How are you feeling today, Whit?"

"Well, I'm sick and tired of being stuck in my bed or on the couch, but it could be worse. How are you doing?"

I told her about Brad's dad and his sister hearing me talk about him.

"So you still love him?"

"I don't know."

"What about the rock-climbing guy?"

"We only had one date."

"And a kiss."

"Okay, and a kiss. I'm not planning on getting back together with Brad, and I'm not planning on dating Tim. I'm just passing time, I guess."

"Passing time? You should be letting loose and making the best of your life. You know it's what Ariel would want. You're too young to pass time as you call it."

"Yeah. It's not that easy though."

"I know, but luckily you have me as a friend. I'm so glad you called because I have an envelope for you to pick up."

"I don't know if I'm feeling up to it today." I drew circles in the dirt on the bridge railing with my finger.

"Perfect! That's why I keep doing this. If you felt like having a good time, I wouldn't need to."

I laughed. "You aren't going to take no for an answer, are you?"

"Absolutely not. Where you at?"

"The bridge by Pine Beach."

"What are you doing there?"

"I just needed a walk."

"Well, walk your butt down to my house then. I'll see you when you get here."

My phone beeped as she hung up. Having a best friend was sure a pain in the butt sometimes, but I did not feel like fighting her on this. I knew this was what I needed.

. . .

135

"MADDY, is that you? You're just in time for dinner," Whitney said from the kitchen.

" Maddy!" Brittany ran into my arms. I squeezed her tight.

She tugged my arm. "Daddy bought me a new Barbie, come see, come see."

"After dinner," Josh said. "Sit down at the table, please."

Whitney was already in her chair, her leg in a cast elevated on a stool under the table. Her crutches were set down next to her chair.

She patted the seat next to her, and I sat down.

"How's your leg?" I said.

"It doesn't hurt as bad as yesterday, but the healing process sucks." She picked up her fork.

"I'm sure it does. Just be patient," Josh said, his hand on hers.

The mashed potatoes and meatloaf with a side of beans was on our plates. When was the last time I made a full meal? Since it was just me now, I had no reason to cook. I lived off fruit cups and frozen veggies. I baked a lot of chicken breasts, too. I did not have much of an appetite since my world turned upside down.

"I know. I just can't wait to get this cast off, that's for sure."

"Me and Mommy are reading *The Little Mermaid* tonight because it was Ariel's favorite, and I miss her," Brittany said with a toothy smile.

I smiled back. My stomach turned at the same time.

"Brittany, eat," Whitney said to distract her.

"It's fine." I leaned close to Brittany, but whispered loud enough for her parents to hear. "I do the same thing. Sometimes when I'm really missing her, I put in the movie."

She smiled back at me.

"Josh, this tastes amazing," Whitney said.

He rubbed her leg.

"I love the cheese in the middle," I said. "So good."

"Why thank you. Usually Whit gets to have all the fun, now I get to try some new cooking."

"Yeah, he's killing me with all the butter," Whitney said with a laugh. "I don't get up enough to work off all these calories.

"You're perfect just the way you are," he said.

Until your family falls apart I wanted to say, but I chewed my food instead.

We had a wonderful dinner, full of laughter and good conversation. Mainly we talked about Brittany's class. We ended the meal with the most delicious homemade apple pie.

"Okay, squirt, time for a bath," Josh said. He picked up Brittany and carried her over his shoulder like a sack of potatoes.

He did it to give Whitney and me some alone time to talk.

"I can't believe Brad is stepping down from his position as a principal."

"I know. That was before everything happened with his dad. If he hadn't, I think the teachers would have rebelled. I feel like I don't even know him anymore, you know?" Sometimes I forgot he was hurting in his own way. I was lost in my own grief.

"Yeah. He's been through a lot. Who do you think will replace him?"

"Who knows. No one could be as bad as the last principal."

"She was a witch," Whitney said. She picked up her crutches.

I followed close behind her as we made our way to the living room. I helped lift her leg onto the sofa and sat down on the chair across from her.

"I'm so sick of not being able to do anything and spending all this time sitting on my butt. She grabbed the familiar pink envelope off the end table next to her. "Here you go."

I took my time opening it. What would it say this time? My heart raced as I unfolded the note. Was I actually excited?

I read it aloud. "Bestie, this letter is a little different from the rest. Ever since we met, you have talked about wanting to do a triathlon. You love to run and swim and bike, but you said you were too nervous to make that commitment. I have signed you up for the Turtleman Triathlon in Shoreview, Minnesota, just north of the cities. You have until July seventeenth to get in shape. Good luck! I wish I could do it with you, but I don't think I'll be fully recovered by then. You've got this, and I'm here for moral support as always! Xo Whit."

I shot her an annoyed look. "Really? You can't just sign me up for my first triathlon without talking to me first."

"Just listen. You know it would be good for you. I actually signed us up to do it together, but that isn't possible now."

I looked at her cast and nodded.

"I've been thinking about this for a long time. It will give you a push to get in shape, and it'll take your mind off everything going on. You can train for it by yourself, or you can find a partner. I'm sure someone from Range Runners would love to train with you."

I nodded. "You're right, training will be a nice distraction, but I wish you had talked to me about this first. I don't know the first thing about training for a triathlon, and I haven't been swimming since high school."

"You'll do great. Brad did a triathlon, didn't he?"

"Yeah, for a bet. That was like five years ago. And he and I aren't exactly on the best of terms."

"You just said you went to his house, and you think you are falling in love with him. Next time talk to him about the triathlon. It will help you find out if there's anything between the two of you. Maybe he can even give you advice so you're more confident about the race."

I glared at her. "I'm sure I can google it."

"You only have a couple weeks of school left, and it's already May. Then no more letters. Please do this for me? For you?"

"But I have letters until July since that's when I have to accomplish this mission."

She laughed. "Oh Maddy, you act like you're going into space. I have to live vicariously through you. You could even put Ariel's name on the back of your shirt when you run."

"This isn't a marathon. I will be running in a swimsuit. I can't put her name on the back."

She tapped on her chin. "I hadn't thought of that. Well, it will be fun. Just sleep on it, okay?"

I laughed. "I do appreciate the thought. I'll think about it, okay? It's just a little surprising, that's all."

"Mommy, I'm ready for the book!" Brittany said with wet hair, all dressed in her Cinderella pajamas.

"I'll let you get back to your family."

"Call me tomorrow." Whitney turned her head to Brittany. "Ask your dad to help Mommy, okay."

"Can I help?" I had my hand on the doorknob.

"No, it's fine. Do you need a ride home?"

"No, I need the walk after this letter."

She laughed. "You'll be fine. Stop over thinking it."

She knew me all too well.

I RAN HERE AND THERE, but I needed to be more consistent. I jumped to the balls of my feet and started at a slow jog. The food bounced around in my stomach, making me ill. Maybe today was not the best day to start running on a regular basis. I'd try again tomorrow. I had a little over two months to get ready for the triathlon.

In the distance, a person ran toward me. When the figure drew closer, his pace slowed to a walk as he stared at me.

I stared back in shock. "Brad?"

"Maddy, is that you? Just out for a walk?"

I shook my head. "When did you start running again?"

His breathing was a little heavy, and he had to catch it. "Well, it's just something I started doing after—you know, everything."

He avoided looking me in the eye, and he seemed to be searching for the right words.

He exhaled more in frustration than to calm his breathing. "The truth is, after I moved out I started running to help with the stress. It helps me think things out, you know?"

I nodded, as if I understood.

He wiped his forehead with the bottom of his shirt, exposing the ripped abs he never had when we were together. I wanted to poke it, see if it was real. He worked out a lot more than he let on. "I thought I saw you running a bit in the distance. Are you starting to run again?"

My face turned red. "Well, I was trying, but then I realized I probably shouldn't run after eating a big dinner."

He smiled and drew my attention to his lips. How foreign they looked now even though I'd kissed those soft lips more times than I could count. And were his teeth always this white? Did he get them bleached? Why couldn't I remember how perfect they were? How perfect he was?

"You're cooking again? That's great."

I looked down. "Not exactly. Whitney invited me over for dinner."

"That's even better. How is she doing now that she's home? I haven't talked to Josh in a couple days."

"Better. Although before she broke her leg she decided it

would be a great idea to sign us up for a triathlon in July and didn't tell me until tonight."

He laughed. "That's great. You will do great."

Our eyes met again, and I could not look away. Even the sparkle in his eyes excited me tonight. I fought the urge to pull him in and kiss him as he wrapped those strong arms around me.

He raised his eyebrows. "Are you okay?"

I felt my face grow warm. What was wrong with me tonight? I shook away the fantasy and cleared my throat. "No, I'm fine. I just ... Do you maybe want to go running with me sometime?"

I obviously caught him off guard, and he was struggling to cover up his shock. "Um, yeah. I'd love that."

"You know I'm not a great runner, so I may slow you down. It's okay if you don't want to."

"Are you kidding me? I would love to run with you and bike and even swim."

He was rambling. Maybe this was a bad idea. He might get the wrong impression. But too late, I'd already asked him. Damn it, Whitney. We were divorced. It's not like he thought I wanted to be with him. I just hoped I could keep my hands off him. Our divorce should have made him fat and ugly. Instead I wanted to slap myself for not realizing how attractive he truly was. Women would be falling all over him any time now. More than just Lisa I'd be worrying about soon enough.

"Let's start with running. You're still an early riser, right?"

"Sure am," he said.

"How about if we try running at five in the morning? Get a nice run in before work?"

"That sounds great."

No, it sounded terrible. The last thing I wanted to do was get up early and run, but I would be too tired if I waited until after work. It was also too easy to come up with an excuse as to why I couldn't run after school. I knew myself.

"See you tomorrow." I walked away from him, but glanced over my shoulder. He was still standing in the same place, staring at me in disbelief.

I turned around. "By the way, how's your dad? Any changes?"

"No, he's still sedated. Mom's staying up there tonight. Security is quite tight so I won't be able to go there for a few days."

'Please keep me updated. I'm thinking of you guys."

He smiled. "Will do. See you bright and early. And, Maddy …"

"Yeah?"

"I'm glad I ran into you."

"Me too."

"This is going to be fun. Just wait. I think you will really enjoy it."

At five in the morning? Did he know me at all?

The grin lingered on his face the whole five-mile run. Was she coming around because she felt bad for him due to his father's health? Or maybe she was starting to forgive him? Or did she need someone to run with, and he happened to be the first person she saw? Whatever the reason, he was grateful. Hopefully, she did not notice how lost he was in her ocean blue eyes? Had he seen her blush or were his eyes deceiving him? Had he imagined the spark between them? More importantly, had she?

He took a cold shower at home and laid out clean running clothes. Though he went to bed early, he had a hard time falling to sleep. He eagerly awaited the morning run.

WHEN HIS ALARM went off at four, he jumped out of bed. Although he hardly slept all night because he couldn't stop thinking about her, he felt amazing and well rested. He walked to her house in the dark at about ten to five and knocked on her door. She answered it right away. Her tight-fitting workout clothes showed how thin she had become.

"I wasn't sure how warm to dress. I haven't been up this early in a long time."

She struggled with securing her armband and phone, so he moved in to help with the Velcro. He felt a bolt of electricity shoot through his body, and he shivered as they touched.

"Thanks," she said.

"Shall we?"

She followed him to the road.

"Do you want to walk a little to warm up and then start jogging?"

She seemed to be thinking about that. "You're the one with the experience. You call the shots and when I'm dying, I'll let you know."

He laughed. "Okay. Let's walk for five minutes, run for five, and keep doing that. If that works okay for you."

"Sounds good to me."

She picked up her pace walking and he followed, stride for stride. His legs were longer than hers, and her steps were much smaller so it took a couple seconds for them to get in sync.

"Are you really leaving the school?"

Her question caught him off guard. Would he even be allowed in the school after everything that happened with Tim? "I don't know. Was I that bad?"

"Well, I don't think Tim's too angry, and the teachers will be fine if you decide to have the spring carnival. I think you need to lighten up a bit, and they will forgive you pretty quick. We're like a big family, most of us anyway. Don't you know you can't mess with teacher's fun day?"

He laughed because she was right.

"You acted like you were trying to get fired."

"Maybe I was." He admitted the truth for the first time. "I bet Tim isn't real happy with me."

"Nah, he's cool with it. I'm sure it's because he ended up laying you out. He told the staff you two were just messing around. I'm glad no one got hurt. Why did you try to hit him anyway? That isn't you."

"I don't know. I guess he rubbed me the wrong way." He would not admit he was jealous, especially when they were finally on speaking terms again. "I can't believe he told them it was staged after I attacked him like that."

"He's a good guy. He doesn't hold it against you."

She said it like she was so close to Tim, and his heart sank. "Okay, time to run. Are you ready?"

"Are you changing the subject on me, Mr. Jones?"

He laughed. "It's Principal Jones."

"Is it?"

They started at a slow jog and she picked it up a bit, to a fast run.

He struggled to keep up.

They slowed the run, and she caught her breath. She started walking backward to look at him while she spoke. "I have a lot of energy. I think I drank a pot of coffee already. I can't believe how beautiful it is out here so early in the morning. No cars, just nature. I can see why you like running so much."

"It clears my head, and Side Lake is so beautiful."

He started running again and she followed.

He glanced at his watch. "Okay, time to walk."

She gasped for breath. "Wow, I'm definitely not as in shape as I thought I was. I just haven't really been consistent with running."

"The first mile is always the hardest. The muscle memory will kick in and you'll just need to retrain your cardio."

There was a chill in the morning air and the trees were bare, but the water was blue and inviting when they ran over the bridge. They spent most of the run silent and enjoying each other's company. It was not weird or awkward like he expected. Once they were on their final walk, she pulled out her phone.

Had she received a text from Tim? He hated to think he would have to be nice to him if he wanted to keep his job or everyone would know it wasn't staged and he tried to hit Tim.

"Do you want to run again tomorrow morning?" Maddy said when his parent's driveway was within view.

"I would love that. Having company while running is fun. Thanks, Maddy."

They passed his driveway and he walked her home.

"See you at school?"

He smiled and watched her walk into her house. She turned back and waved with a small smile. He waved back before turning around.

LISA GREETED him as he walked into the school.

"Good morning, Mr. Jones. I'm so glad you came back. I heard about your dad. How is he?"

"He's still sedated, but doing much better. Thank you. Can you come into my office for a second?"

"Sure."

She followed him into his office, and he shut the door. "I want to apologize for my behavior the other day."

"Canceling the spring carnival and trying to quit on us? Oh, don't you worry. We all know you were going through a lot. I'm sure it isn't easy. I'm not going to lie, I was pretty angry, and then the whole set up with Tim, I thought you were actually trying to hit him. He told us the staged fight was his idea." She raised her eyebrows at him. "But you guys should not roughhouse in school. Please don't do it again, you almost gave me a heart attack."

"Will do. I'm sorry we worried everyone."

"It's forgotten." She hesitated. "I would like to bake you and your family some cookies. I'm sure no one has time or energy for cooking. It's the least I can do."

He shook his head. "That is very thoughtful. They only let two visitors in the hospital so I had to sneak in to see him a couple times. I don't think I'll be there today unless he takes a turn for the worse."

"Well, just let me know if you need anything, okay? Don't forget I have a hot tub if you need to relax." She ran her hand up his arm.

He cleared his throat and moved away. "I'd better get going. Cafeteria duty." He walked away and glanced over his shoulder to find her busy checking out his backside. She made everything so uncomfortable.

He stopped in the break room to grab a cup of coffee after the kids were in their classrooms. Lisa followed him in and stood behind him as he poured his coffee. He sat down at the table with the list of decorations from the spring carnival.

She looked over his shoulder and pointed at the list. "Would you like me to help you with the list?"

"That would be great. I know Maddy took care of most of this, but there are a couple of games I need to make sure we have the stuff for. Like the bowling pins."

She started rubbing his shoulders. He stiffened at her touch.

"You are so tense. Just relax."

She would be angry if he sent her away, and his job was relying on her help, so he relaxed his shoulders and tried his best to enjoy the massage. His shoulders were stiff.

"Also, the tic-tac-toe board. I'm not sure where they keep it or if we still have it."

She moved her hands down his back and arms. "You have such strong arms. You must work out."

Was she really here to help him? He shrugged her off and moved away from her, but she just followed and stood by his side.

"Will you be home around five? I'll make those cookies right after school and drop them off."

"Sounds good," he said. He did not eat cookies, but he knew she wouldn't take no for an answer. It was thoughtful of her, but he wondered what her intentions were. He walked out into the hallway and left so he did not have to kick her out of his office. She would never leave on her own.

THE DAY WENT BETTER than he planned. He made an apology speech during both lunches for the teachers. They were all understanding thanks to Lisa telling them about his father.

"Take all the time you need," one teacher said, and they all agreed.

After lunch, he went in search of Tim, who had not shown up in the break room during his lunch. He may not like the guy, but if it wasn't for what Tim said, the teacher's wouldn't have been so forgiving.

Tim was laminating hand-colored flowers at the little table in his classroom.

He forced a friendly smile. "Tim."

"Principal Jones," he said. "To what do I owe the pleasure?"

He kept laminating and only glanced up once or twice.

"Looks like you learned how to laminate, huh? I still don't know how to use one of those things."

Tim looked up. "Maddy taught me."

Tim sounded a bit bitter. The guy hadn't covered for him out of the goodness of his heart. He did it for Madeline or for some other reason, and he was about to find out. "I want to apologize for my behavior the other day."

"Oh, you mean when you tried to hit me?"

He clenched his jaw. "Yeah, about that--"

"You were jealous, I know. Although you forgot you're old and slow. Did you think I would actually let you hit me? Ha!"

"What?"

"Madeline is a catch, and from what I hear you two used to be married. You were threatening me, marking your territory. Am I right?"

"I was angry. I hope you will accept my apology," he said through clenched teeth. This was so hard to do.

Tim put down his artwork and stood up. "Listen, I told everyone we staged the scuffle because I'm looking out for Madeline. She asked so I did it. I'm not going to stop seeing her, just so you know."

He closed his gaping mouth. The nerve of this guy. Who did he think he was? Coming into his school and trying to tell him what to do? Not a chance.

Tim was standing with his chest all puffed out. "Listen, I know you don't like me and to be honest, the feeling is mutual. But I care about Maddy, and I think it would be best if you stayed away from us. Let her be happy."

He clenched his fists at his sides. He wanted to punch Tim in the face, but he needed to maintain self-control. This jerk was obviously trying to get him going and it was working, but he would lose Maddy forever if he lost control again.

"If she decides she wants to be with you, that's her choice. No matter what, I'm your boss and you need to be professional at school. I highly doubt you're her type, and surprisingly she didn't mention you when we were running together this morning."

Rubbing it in a bit and the expression on Tim's face was

worth it. Before Tim had a chance to say anything, he turned to leave.

"Have a great day, Tim. Thank you for having my back." He could not wait until the school year was over, and he never had to see that punk again.

He passed Maddy's room. The door was open, and she was walking out. She almost crashed into him.

Her eyes lit up and she smiled. "Brad, how did it go with the teachers? I'm on my way to retrieve my next class from the cafeteria. Want to walk and talk?"

"I was heading that way anyway," he said. "It went well. No one wants me to leave after all."

"Like I said, we're a family here. They love you, you know that. Plus, they would never find a principal like you. When you were promoted, everyone was so relieved. I never thought I'd say this, but you're a really great boss when you aren't being a prick."

He laughed at her bluntness. "Well, thank you. I even apologized to your friend, Tim."

"He's not so bad, is he?"

He tried to read her expression. Was she trying to see if he accepted Tim? Did she really like this guy? He hated to think about it, but it was none of his business anymore. He had so many questions for her, but he wasn't going to push it and risk ruining this new relationship they were building back up.

"He seems great. I know you had some part in all of this, so thank you."

She winked at him. "You know I've got your back."

"I appreciate it. How are you doing today?"

"Well, I'm a little tired from the run this morning, but I can't wait to do it again tomorrow. Thank you, for running with me."

"It's my pleasure."

Her attention was on the open lunchroom where her next class was impatiently waiting for her arrival. "See you in the morning?"

"See you in the morning."

He could stand there all day talking to her. He missed their conversations and the way her face lit up when she was passionate about something. He wanted to do something special to show her how much he appreciated her. He had the perfect idea in mind to make her forget about Tim and show her he was still the man for her, despite their past.

I was shelving the last of the books when Tim walked in the door.

"Hey there, Ms. Librarian. I hardly saw you all day. How are you doing?"

"Good. I went for a run this morning, and I feel amazing. I'm not going to lie, I'm a little tired from waking up so early, but it was worth it. Whitney signed me up for a triathlon in two months so I'm trying to get in shape."

"That's impressive. Where is the triathlon?"

"It's in Shoreview, southern Minnesota, by the Cities. She actually signed us both up, but with her broken leg, I'm afraid I'm doing my first triathlon alone."

"Have you ever completed a triathlon before?"

"No, have you?"

"I usually do one a year. Are you a swimmer?"

"Not since like the tenth grade," I said with a laugh. "That was a long time ago. I hope it's like riding a bike. I used to live for swimming."

"I think you'll do just fine. Where are you training for the swimming?"

Crap. I didn't think about that. The lakes were too cold to swim in right now. Was there a pool this town? "I'm not really sure."

"You should come to the YMCA with me this weekend in Virginia."

"I guess I could do that. Yeah. Thank you."

He would probably swim circles around me, but oh well. As long as I did not embarrass myself too much.

"Maybe we could have breakfast after and take a little run around the lakes in town? Might be fun to make a day of it."

"I have nothing going on. Let's do it."

I STOPPED to see Whitney on my way home. She seemed so happy to have a visitor.

"I'm so glad you're having fun with this," Whitney said after I told her I was going swimming with Tim, and I had a great run with Brad. "And I'm glad you and Brad are finally talking."

"Me too. I have to admit, I'm a little worried about how Brad is going to take it when he finds out I'm swimming with Tim."

"Brittany, put that down. It's time to brush your teeth." She turned back to me. "Sorry about that. Britt's been struggling since I can't move around as much. That girl thinks she can get away with everything. What were we saying? Oh yeah, Brad with the Tim thing. I think it's great you're getting back in the pool with Tim and running with Brad."

"I guess. They've both been so helpful. It's not like I plan on having a relationship with either one of them."

Whitney laughed. "Girl, both of them have a crush on you. It must be so hard having two hot men fighting over you."

"Brad does not have a crush on me. He's my ex-husband

for a reason, and Tim, it's just fun. Sure, we kissed that one time, but that was just a moment of weakness on both our parts."

"I hate missing all of this."

"Consider yourself lucky."

"Mom," Brittany said.

Whitney's head snaped back, she looked exhausted.

"Let me put her to bed," I said.

She hesitated. "No, you don't need to do that."

"Whitney, I'd love to. I miss her and we really bonded. Please, let me have some time with her."

Her face relaxed. "If you're sure."

"I am." And I meant every word. I loved my time with her and after I read her a book, I fell asleep snuggling in bed with her.

Josh woke me up when he got home. He had been working late. He walked me to the door. Whitney had already fallen asleep on the couch. I heard her snoring from the hallway.

"It was really nice of you to help out. I hate when I have to work late and leave her alone to take care of everything."

"I'm glad I can help. I'm pretty much just sitting home alone in my gigantic, empty house so if you ever need me to help, just let me know."

"You know, Whitney is so happy to see you so happy. She was really worried about you. And you know who else was really worried about you?"

"Have a great night, Josh," I said putting my hand on his shoulder before I turned around and walked out the door.

THE WEEK WAS QUITE busy and went by fast. The teachers and children were getting spring fever. This was the time of year when the kids became rambunctious and did not want to stay indoors so the teachers took them outside as much as they could on the nice days.

Brad seemed back to his normal self, and we were running more than walking. Every morning he was at my door before five o'clock, and I was so proud of myself for getting out of bed. Knowing someone was counting on me to do so helped. Without having that accountability, I'd likely snooze my alarm clock.

We chatted a lot about school stuff and the spring carnival. We were finally becoming friends again. Although seeing him in his tight athletic clothes made me swoon, I kept it professional between us, and he was a total gentlemen.

By Friday morning my shin splints were getting worse. I was afraid if I told Brad, he would make me take a break from running every day, and I was in such a good routine with working out now.

I heard a weird noise outside. I opened the door and found him hanging off the railing of my deck doing pull ups.

"What are you doing?"

He dropped down and wiped his hands on his pants. "I like to do some pull-ups and push-ups before we run, it's just a thing I do to get my blood pumping. I usually knock after I'm done."

"Impressive," I said with a nod. It truly was. "I never realized this before. You keep surprising me. I feel like I don't know you at all."

"Is that a good thing or a bad thing?"

We made our way down the driveway.

"It's a good thing. You're so ambitious. It's weird because I thought I knew you so well, and then you go and get all ripped. It's just different, that's all."

He shot me a smile that made my heart skip a beat.

"You're looking pretty good yourself."

I was suddenly all giddy like a teenager around him,

which was so strange since I had been married to this man for all those years. I never felt nervous about him, comfortable was more the word I would have used. Was that because I couldn't have him whenever I wanted him anymore? How would I react when he started dating?

"Do you think us hanging out all the time and training is a bad idea?" I silently hoped he would say no.

"Rather than us hating each other and never talking? Not at all. Are you having second thoughts?"

"No. Just curious."

He picked up his pace to a jog, and I followed. "I do have something to tell you."

"Let me go first," he said. "I signed up for the Turtleman Triathlon, too. I hope you don't mind. I thought that since we're training together, maybe it would be fun. I haven't done a race in, well you know how long. I just thought I might as well. Is that okay?"

I thought about it. It didn't bother me the smallest bit that he wanted to race with me, but I needed to tell him about Tim. If he became possessive, I would have to tell him no.

"That's totally fine. It's not like we would actually be able to run it together. The men and women compete separately, don't they?"

"Yeah, but I would be there cheering you on."

"I'd like that," I said. "I was talking to Tim about my triathlon the other day, and he wants me to swim with him at the YMCA."

I held my breath, which was really hard to do, waiting for his reply.

"Go for it. You don't need to ask for my permission. As long as you don't stop training with me."

I sighed. He seemed sincere. He didn't look angry at all. "Oh, great. I was worried you would be upset. I know you don't exactly like him."

"No, no. We had a misunderstanding. I'm glad you're doing things, getting out. I was really worried about you."

"You don't need to worry about me."

"When are you guys going to the Y?"

"This afternoon. We were supposed to go in the morning, but I told him I needed to relax a little after our run before I went swimming."

"That was probably a good call."

He slowed down to a walk.

"Can we run a little longer? My lungs feel good, I'm not having a hard time catching my breath, and my legs aren't hurting one bit right now."

"Let's do it," he said catching up. "Have your legs been hurting pretty bad?"

"My legs always hurt a little on the front, but it's not too bad right now."

A car came at us and we had to move onto the shoulder of the road. Brad slipped in front of me, and I stared at his backside. He had on a tight long-sleeve Nike shirt and gray wind pants to match. I could see the ripples in his shoulders and the V-shape from his shoulders to his lower back. I took a good look at his butt before he moved next to me. I resisted the urge to squeeze it. His thick hair was sexy and wind-blown, thick unlike many men his age.

He was back running next to me. We were both quiet, just taking in nature around us. When we were a few blocks from home we slowed to a walk.

"How are you feeling?"

"Just a little pressure on the front of my legs, but other than that, great."

"Sounds like some pretty bad shin splints. You may need to get some new shoes."

"You think that will help?"

"If not, we'll do some other adjustments. Can we go inside? I'll check out your legs ."

"Of course. Sorry, it's a little messy." A little messy? Brad was the one who always cooked and cleaned. Since he left, I never got into the rhythm of doing it all. Until recently, I had a hard time even getting off the couch, then the mess of my life kept me busy.

I led him into the living room, and he sat down next to me on the couch. I tried to pull up my running pants, but they were too tight.

"Let me run and change my pants."

I came back in a pair of shorts. He crouched down in front of me and massaged the muscles around my shin.

"Does this hurt?"

His touch was warm, and his gentleness had me imagining him naked instead of focusing on the pain in my legs.

I told him where the pain was while daydreaming about tackling him on the floor. What was wrong with me? It seemed normal for me to want my marriage back after the divorce was final, but it would never work between us. Too much had happened.

"How about here? Does it hurt when I push here?"

"A little bit. It mainly hurts when I'm running. Out of nowhere, shooting pain."

"I have a trick that works, but it isn't easy. Would you try an ice bath? It's terrible at first, but it really helps."

I wanted to keep running without pain so I would try anything at this point. An ice bath couldn't be that bad. "Yeah, I'm in. What do you need me to do?"

He ran a cold bath and I brought up two bags of ice from the freezer. He took them from me and poured them in the bathtub.

"What do you have on underneath your shirt?"

My face grew hot, but I did not lose eye contact. This

man has seen me naked so many times, so why was I feeling so bashful just thinking about him mentioning what was under my shirt?

I cleared my throat. "A sports bra."

He put his hands on both sides of the bottom of my shirt. His face was now just a whisper away, his lips close to mine. I could feel his warm breath on me.

"May I?"

His words made me warm all over. I nodded, our eyes now locked. He pulled my shirt over my head and our gaze came back together, the passion more intense. I felt goose bumps break out all over my body as his eyes studied me.

I leaned in to kiss him, giving into the temptation. I wanted to relieve all the tension. I needed to feel his lips on mine. Needed to know if this passion could be any more intense than it was already becoming. Was it possible after all these years for it to suddenly be this intense?

Instead, he turned his back and grabbed a towel. Our eyes still locked, he led me to the bathtub.

"It's going to be really cold at first, but once you get in you'll numb up fast. I'll teach you some belly breathing. It's also a great way to practice strengthening your mind for pain during the triathlon. Your mind needs to be as strong as your body.

I stripped off my socks and put one foot in. I wasn't going to remind him that I'd been through child birth because it would ruin the moment we were having.

The ice-cold water took my breath away.

"It's not that bad," I said after a moment. I put my other foot in and the coldness burned my skin. I pulled my foot out.

"This will help, trust me. You have to get used to the water."

I did as I was told.

"Now look at me and breathe from your stomach. When you breathe in, stick out your stomach and when you exhale, bring your stomach back in. Practice as you slowly sink deeper into the bath until you're sitting down on the bottom of the tub with your legs out.

I took in each breath loudly, focusing on my breathing and looking at the water. "How can cold burn this bad?"

"Focus." He held onto my arm to keep me steady. "Now look into my eyes, not at the water."

I was glad he told me to look into his eyes because there was no place I'd rather look. My butt dropped into the water, and I could no longer breathe. All the oxygen was sucked out of my lungs as it took my breath away.

"Look at me," he said.

I followed his lead with my deep breaths until my legs were straight out. The feeling was horrible, but the breathing helped. "How long do I have to sit in here?"

"Until my alarm goes off."

He massaged my shoulders and arms. He sat on the side of the bathtub and blocked me from seeing the water. I found myself holding my breath again. Everything was numb, but he took me through some mediation by focusing on colors.

Once his alarm finally went off, I jumped up and splashed him.

"That's freezing cold," he said with a laugh. I picked up an ice cube and slid it down the back of his shirt after he helped me out of the bathtub and put a towel around me.

He jumped around the bathroom, pulling out his shirt.

"So cold," he said.

I smirked. "Use your breathing techniques."

He shook his head and flashed me his sexy grin.

He came at me, and I held out my hands defensively. My legs were bright red and still numb.

"You're lucky you're all wet and numb or I would tickle you."

I laughed. "So cold," I said, my body tense. I couldn't help but flirt with him.

He grabbed another towel and wrapped it around my upper body. He picked me up like a bride and carried me to the couch.

"I could get used to this," I said with a laugh.

He placed me on the couch with such gentleness and wrapped his arms around me.

I wanted to cuddle with him like that forever. He ran his fingers through my hair, and I slouched down to a more comfortable position.

"I miss this so much," he said.

"Me too." I closed my eyes and relaxed. My legs were so cold, they felt hot, but the light touch of his hand on my skin and in my hair kept me from thinking about the cold.

I dozed off for a few minutes, but woke when he tried to sneak out from behind me. I sat up to let him out. Touching me had turned him on, the evidence pressed against my back and was hard to miss.

His eyes followed mine, and he turned away very fast. When he turned back, his face was pink, and he looked so cute and nervous. He dug his fingers into his eyes. "I should get going. I'm sorry about that."

I stepped closer to him, and he stood there, frozen. I took another step toward him until our noses were practically touching. I wrapped my arms around him, and I pressed my lips to his.

A spark shot through my body, and my heart fluttered in my chest. Our connection was not gone. If anything, I wanted him, needed him more than ever.

My fingers dug into his shoulders and made their way up

161

his shirt. He grabbed my hands and the world seemed to stop. I held my breath.

"Are you sure?" he whispered.

I nodded and pulled my sports bra over my head.

He stared at me, as if he'd never seen me naked before. I grabbed him and kissed him with all the passion in my soul. I did not care about the consequences. I wanted him, needed him right now. We took off our clothes until we both stood there, naked.

He grabbed my chin in his hand.

"I've missed you so much. Missed this."

I pressed my frozen body against his warm skin. I couldn't wait another minute to make love to this man. He picked me up and I wrapped my legs around him, kissing him everywhere I could reach until he lay me down on the bed where we'd made love so many times in the past.

This time there was no comparison. It was by far the best sex we ever had until the second round. Maybe that was the best sex we ever had.

He stared at the ceiling, replaying the morning over and over in his head as she lay there sleeping with her head on his chest. His arm was around her naked body. She was so beautiful, her body so smooth and perfect.

In all the years they had been together, the sex had never been that amazing. This passion between them was on a whole new level. He'd dreamed of this moment with her and thought it was never going to happen again. He was sure she hated him, but she was here with him after the most amazing and passionate sex of his life.

Her head lifted off his chest, and she turned to look at him. He worried about what her reaction would be, but she just smiled at him.

"That was the best sex we've ever had," she said.

He laughed out loud. Those were the exact words he was thinking over and over in his head.

"I've been thinking the same thing. I can't stop thinking about it."

She sat up and covered her body with the white sheet. "I hope this doesn't make things weird between us."

He tried to understand where she was coming from, but he just got more confused. "It won't."

"You'll still run with me?" She turned her back to him and reached down for her towel.

He grabbed his clothes laying on the floor next to the bed. Being in the bed they slept in together for all those years felt so strange, yet so familiar.

"Of course. There is nothing I'd rather do. I love spending time with you."

"I just don't want this to ruin the new friendship we've finally built."

Was she dumping him? Telling him the sex was the best sex she's ever had, but also never going to happen again?

He held his shirt in his hands. "What does this mean for us, then?"

She avoided looking him in the eye. She kept staring at his chest, and he smiled at her obvious admiration.

She caught the grin. "I'm sorry, but it's like this isn't even your chest I'm looking at. You have a whole new body, it's hard not to stare."

He laughed, flexing his chest for her.

"Stop it and put your shirt on. I can't be serious when you're looking like that." She traced the line that started between his hips and disappeared under his underwear. She turned away in frustration.

He pulled his shirt over his head. "Maddy, what does this mean? We've been through so much together and--"

"We need to act as if it never happened. Obviously we had a lot of sexual frustration between us, but we divorced for a reason. I don't want to lose you. We finally have this great friendship." She sighed. "This is all my fault."

He hugged her tight. "Don't regret what happened. Let's just take it one day at a time."

"I can't. This can't happen again. We're friends. We can't let a moment of weakness make us forget everything."

The sadness was back in her eyes.

He lifted her chin with his hand and kissed her with sadness in his heart. He in no way wanted to frustrate her anymore. This was obviously very hard for her to process.

When he opened his eyes, her eyes were open as well. "I understand, but I needed that. I respect you and your decision, but I will never stop loving you."

Her eyes blurred with tears. He needed to leave before she started to panic and said things she didn't mean out of fear. At the door, he turned back to look at her one more time. She was glowing, and her hair was a mess in a very sexy, I just got laid kind of way. He took a mental snapshot and smiled before walking out the door and wondering if she would ever invite him to step foot in their house again.

AS SOON AS he turned onto Turtle Creek Road from her driveway, he saw a black Jeep.

Tim rolled down his passenger side window and leaned over the seat.

"Brad, what are you doing over here?"

He wanted to tell him exactly why he was at Maddy's house and piss the guy off, but instead he said, "We went for a run this morning. You picking her up to go swimming?"

A smug grin appeared on Tim's face. He stopped himself, but he wanted nothing more than to tell Tim he had to go home and shower because he just made love to his Madeline.

"Have a good time."

"Oh, we will."

B rad walked down the hall on Monday just after lunch. He met Tim in the hall as he was getting ready to shut his door.

They stared at each other, but no words were exchanged. Brad wondered how their swim date went. Why was he the one jealous even though he was the one lucky enough to make love to her? He knew she would never sleep with them both in the same day. She slept with him for a reason, and he was not going to let her off thinking they were just friends. Friends definitely didn't make love like that.

Tim shut his door but not before shooting Brad that cocky grin, almost challenging him.

He continued to walk to his office and saw Lisa behind him, picking up her pace to catch him.

"Brad, wait."

"Good afternoon, Lisa. What can I do for you today?"

"I was wondering if you could help me move some boxes in my room. I'm trying to decorate for spring, and the box I need is really heavy and up high on the cupboard."

"Why don't you just ask the janitor for help?"

"He's busy and I need it done right now. Please, for me?"

He hated her flirty tone and liked to think she just needed the help, but he was unsure. Whenever he tried to be nice to her, she always touched him in a way that made his skin crawl, or she laughed for absolutely no reason.

"No problem," he said.

He followed her into her empty room. The box was so high he had to get a chair to reach it. He set it on the counter and opened it for her.

"Thank you. It's so great having a strong guy around here to help us ladies out. Can you help me put some of these up? If you aren't too busy?"

How could he say no now? He would put up a couple decorations and make his escape. The janitor would have been a much better fit for this job.

"Sure, I can help out for a couple of minutes, but I have to get back to my office. I have a busy day today."

"Any help would be great. Thanks, Brad. You're just so strong and tall, I knew you would be the perfect man for the job."

She put him to work on the back wall, pinning up decorations while she directed where they went.

"Funny how much faster this goes with two people. Are you feeling any better about the other day?"

She meant no harm and he did have a few minutes to spare. She seemed so lonely sometimes. Was the persona she put on all an act so she didn't look as vulnerable as she was.

"It hasn't been easy. I feel terrible for the way I acted in those meetings. Thank you for being so understanding. You've been there for me through this horrible last year. You've invited me over for meals, cooked for me, and I'm sorry it has taken me this long to tell you thank you." It needed to be said. Sure, she was way too flirty and always wanted his attention, but she was struggling and people had a hard time getting close to her due to her strong personality.

She beamed at him. "I've always cared about you, Brad, and with everything that happened I want you to know I'm your friend and I'm here for you. I'd love to have you over for dinner one of these nights again."

Maybe he had been misreading her all this time. Maybe Maddy was wrong when she said Lisa had a crush on him. She really did care about him as a friend. Maybe she just didn't have any real friends. People followed her lead because they were scared of her, not because they actually liked her. How lonely she must be. And she felt bad about what happened to Ariel.

"I would love to take you up on that."

"How about Friday night? I'll get some cabernet and we can sit by the bonfire and chat. It'll be fun."

"That sounds great. I'll be there. Thank you."

"At times like these, you need to surround yourself with friends. I care about you."

ON FRIDAY MORNING, he met Maddy on the way to her house.

"Look at you all up and ready, meeting me half way."

"I just feel so full of energy today. Our morning runs are starting to grow on me. How is your dad doing? Were they able to leave the breathing tube out yesterday?"

"Yes, actually. He's having a hard time speaking, but it's finally out and he's awake. His voice is all dry and scratchy. He's been a bit crabby. My sister warned the nurses before he got the breathing tube out that he might be a bit difficult to deal with. You know how my dad can get sometimes."

"Yes, I do. That sums him up pretty well," she said with a laugh.

They picked up the pace to a slow jog.

"Is he going to be okay?"

If only he knew the answer. "I'm not sure, to be honest. I wonder if he will ever be the same again."

The nurses had told him his father was having flashbacks from Vietnam that were now becoming nightmares.

"He seems to forget who he is. The hospital has finally given us the okay for me to visit. My sister is staying with him tonight, and I will be staying with him tomorrow night."

He lost his breath, likely because of what he had to tell her. "I had a nice chat with Lisa the other day."

Her pace slowed next to him. She cleared her throat. "Oh, really?"

He knew that tone, the one she had when they were married and she was angry at him for doing or not doing something. It started off with a twitch in her eye as the anger bubbled to the surface, and he would wait for her to explode. It did not happen often, but when he pushed her too far she would either lose her temper or take off without saying another word.

"After I went off at the faculty and pretty much resigned and they all let me back without issue, I felt like I needed to go the extra mile to let them know I do want to be there so I helped her with some decorations in her room."

She nodded.

He was still in the doghouse. He needed to find a way to make her understand where he was coming from.

"Mmm hmm."

Oh, if he had any doubt she was angry, she just confirmed it. Maddy and Lisa used to be friends, but he had forgotten why they ended up hating each other so much.

"Anyway, she invited me over tonight for a bonfire after work."

She picked up her pace, and he struggled to catch up because he was holding his breath as he waited for her to answer. Only she did not say anything. She just kept running. He stayed a couple feet behind her, staring at the ground. Had he screwed it all up? He was such an idiot.

She started walking at a fast pace, still in front of him.

"Maddy?"

She did not answer, so he said her name twice more.

"What? I'm just focused," she said with definite anger in her voice. Her arms swung faster at her sides, and her hands were in fists.

"Are you mad at me?" Dumb question.

He had to say it, even though he knew she would say she was not mad. Women always said they weren't angry but they really were. Why did they confuse men like that? As if we were blind and could not see they were obviously upset.

"No. I mean, I'm just surprised after everything she did to me that you are such good friends with her."

"I'm sorry, I didn't mean to--"

"No, it's fine." She pushed ahead of him again. "You don't owe me anything. We aren't married anymore."

Well, this conversation sure turned for the worst fast. He could not cancel on Lisa at the last minute, and he needed to show he was grateful she had his back or she could easily influence everyone to let him go. He deserved it.

"It's not like that. I just thought--"

She turned around fast and stared into his eyes. Was she going to yell and stomp off? Instead her eyes filled with tears.

"I'm totally overacting and I'm so sorry. I don't own you. Let's talk about the elephant in the room. We slept together, and we've both been too nervous to talk about it."

He watched a tear slide down the side of her nose. He wiped it away with his gloved thumb.

Her beautiful mouth curved into a small smile.

He did not regret it. He wanted them to be together again. To hold her at night. To tell her how much he loved her. To tell their favorite Ariel stories and never forget her, together. To celebrate how much they love her, together.

"It was a mistake."

His heart ached at her words. All the air sucked from his lungs.

"I appreciate you running with me, but I think it needs to stop now. We need some distance."

He hung his head. "Is this because of Lisa? I'll cancel, just say the word. I didn't mean to upset you."

She put her hand on his arm. "No, no. I was just frustrated, and I've been avoiding you all week and then when you said Lisa, for some reason it set things off in my head. I'm not mad at you. But I think we need some space, okay? We divorced for a reason, and we have to see each other every day at school, and we run together."

"I don't want us to stop running together," he said. "Please."

"How about if we run on Wednesday mornings together? I think it would be good for me to start running more on my own. I'm starting to swim, and I'm doing some biking on the weekends."

"Whatever you need," he said.

"Brad, I canceled swimming with Tim last weekend after we … you know. I was just so overwhelmed with what it all meant and what could even come from all of this. I'm torn and I just need a little space."

"I'm sorry you feel this way. You can talk to me."

"There is nothing to talk about. I did reschedule, and I'm

still going swimming with him. Just give me some space to clear my head, okay?"

He was careful not to look too disappointed. "Whatever you need."

"Thank you for being such a great person. I have to go, okay?"

She walked away, leaving him with an ill feeling. What just happened? Did he miss something?

22

I met Tim at the YMCA in Virginia at six in the morning. The pool was not as cold as I expected, but my swimsuit from the early 2000's was way too tight and pinched my arm pits. Note to self: buy a new swimsuit.

Tim jumped in and stared up at me from the pool.

"You coming?"

I pulled my hair into a tight bun and jumped in the lane next to him. I had not been swimming in a pool since the tenth grade when I dropped out of swimming. I meant to, I just never got around to it.

I put on my googles and dove under the water.

"You don't have a swim cap?"

I shook my head. "I'll be fine."

"Okay," he said, obviously not believing me.

I hardly needed a swim cap just to do a few laps.

"Let's do a practice lap. Swim to the end of the pool and back and then you can rest. You up for that?"

I laughed because it was only fifty yards. I did like twenty-five hundred yards a practice in high school. "Let's do it."

I dove under the water and pushed off the wall. My arms ached more with each stroke I took, and my legs would not kick right. Even though I'd securely put my hair back, it kept blocking my vision as strands flew in my face.

I was halfway down the pool when Tim passed me coming back already. What a show off. His stroke looked so smooth, flawless as he breathed every third stroke.

Once I was within an arms' reach of the wall, I bent at the waist and completed a flip turn. Swimming was like riding a bike, you never really forget. I surfaced and gasped for air, then continued my slow pace, arms almost numb as I finally touched the wall and stood up.

Tim was smiling at me as I pushed my hair back.

"You looked pretty good. Ready for a hundred now?"

"A hundred yards? You go ahead. I'll catch up."

I spent the rest of the time taking a lot of breaks and trying to catch my breath. I stretched every time I hit the wall. I forgot how exhausting swimming was until now.

I showered and changed. My whole body was weak and exhausted. The swimming portion of the triathlon would be hard, but I was not giving up. My hair was so tangled it took me forever to brush out the snarls. I would never make the mistake of swimming laps without a swim cap again. I thought about all the times Brad would sit behind me and brush my hair when the snarls were too much for me to comb through. He separated my hair into sections and carefully brushed through with such focus to not to pull too hard. I missed that so much.

Tim was waiting patiently outside the door when I exited the locker room. "Did you have fun?"

I grimaced. "I'm in quite a bit of pain, but I would do it again if that's what you're asking."

"How about tomorrow morning?"

"Too soon. Next week, maybe."

He laughed. "Anyway I could convince you to go out to dinner with me tonight?"

The sweet look of hope in his eyes had me hesitating. "Yes."

He'd been asking me for days, and I kept saying no because of my feelings for Brad. We slept together, and I had a hard time getting him off my mind. I did not hop into bed with just anyone, and the sex was so much better than we ever had. It was intense and new and ... A flash of heat hit my face, and I tried to stop thinking about that night, but it was a struggle. The way his muscles moved, the gentleness in his touch. The electrifying feeling every time we touched.

I could not get the thought of him and Lisa out of my mind. I hated that she thought she had a chance with him. Was I a terribly selfish person for feeling that way? But it hurt too bad every time I was with him. Thinking about going on with our lives together without Ariel, as if she never existed? I could not do it. Every time I looked at him, I thought about Ariel, and how the three of us would never be together again. Our journey together was over, and we both needed to move on. I just hoped he would not move on too soon or with Lisa.

I dressed casual and tried so hard to distract myself from thinking about Brad and Lisa being together tonight at her stupid bonfire, but it was all I could think about. I twirled my mascara brush over my lashes. The brush slipped and went right into my eye. I was a hot mess. I had a smudge of mascara on my eyeball, which now watering and running down my face in perfect black streaks.

The doorbell rang. I grabbed a washcloth and wiped away the smudges on my cheeks and black shadows under my eyes. I looked as if I had two black eyes. Damn Brad, get out of my head.

I opened the door and Tim smiled at me.

"Hey, come on in. I forgot something upstairs. I'll just be a minute."

I washed away the black and redid my concealer and then smiled at myself in the mirror. I looked maybe a little too thin, but I loved how I looked in these pants. Did Brad notice? I had to stop thinking about Brad and give Tim my full attention, but it was so hard. I could do this. I let out a loud exhale and one more quick glance in the mirror before returning downstairs.

I grabbed a light coat even though it was almost seventy degrees today. May in Minnesota was unpredictable.

Tim was sweeping my kitchen floor when I finally came down.

"Okay, first you do my dishes, and now you're sweeping my floor. You better be careful or I'll expect you to do this for me every time you come over." I meant it as a joke, but his smile made me realize that was exactly what he was hoping for.

"Then maybe you need to start inviting me over more."

He opened the car door for me and shut it when I got in. He could not seem to take his eyes off me. I felt my face grow hot so I stared out the window and nervously began a conversation. "How was your day?"

"Good," he said. "I extended the lease on my rental until the end of July so I can teach summer school at the high school."

"Oh, really? Is that what you want to be? A high school teacher?"

"I prefer teaching elementary school, but it's just a summer gig. I wanted to get some experience to put on my resume. I'm really hoping to get on in the Hibbing school district."

"Teaching jobs aren't always easy to find. Good for you."

"How is your friend doing?"

"She'll be back in the fall." I said, a little bit ruder than I meant to.

He put up the hand that wasn't on the steering wheel in surrender.

We pulled into the restaurant right off the river. Riverside was one of my favorite places to dine and where Brad and I held our wedding reception years ago. The restaurant was not large, but elegant and lights on the waterfall outside shone in purple, red, and green. Our wedding had a Hawaiian theme with lei's and real palm trees from Florida. Thank goodness for my awesome aunt who somehow shipped them all the way to Minnesota. The weather was perfect and sunny, the band was amazing, and the food was flawless. That was one of the best days of my life.

Brad and I were on top of the world that day. I was never scared or had second thoughts like people warned me I would. Brad was my best friend, and the love of my life. I could not imagine my life without him in it back then. That was before we had Ariel, of course. Before she was born or taken from us too soon. I still wondered what I did to deserve the pain of losing my baby girl. Some days I wanted to swear at the sky, announce my hate for whatever higher power took a child from her mother.

I looked up to see Tim studying me. "Everything okay?"

I opened the menu. "Yeah, it's fine."

We ordered, but he was still trying to read me. "Can I ask you a question?"

I PUSHED my hair behind my shoulders. "Sure."

"Who is that little girl in the picture at your house? Do you and Brad have a daughter?"

I thought back to the last dinner Tim and I shared when I

ran out of the restaurant. "We did, but she passed away almost a year ago now."

His mouth dropped and he did not even blink. I may have caught him a little off-guard.

"Sorry, I guess that was a little blunt."

"I just ... I just ... I'm so sorry to hear that. Everything makes so much sense now. Why there was the sexual frustration between you and Brad. The reason you ran out at our last dinner date. Why you're so jumpy. I can't imagine what the two of you are going through, and here I am pushing to go out with you. The kiss ... I'm so embarrassed." He covered his face with his hand.

I lifted his hand away from his face. "It's okay, there is nothing between us anymore. We're divorced. I should have told you. This is on me."

"Here I took you swimming because I was so jealous about the two of you running together. I am such an idiot."

"No, I am. I'm sorry. I shouldn't have kept this from you. But I liked that you didn't know my past. That you didn't feel sorry for me. You don't understand the way people look at me when they find out about her. I liked that someone in my life didn't know. If I had told you, you never would have wanted to go out with me. You would be giving me looks of pity like you are right now."

"I'm just a little caught off guard here. You're right, you should have told me. You're the horrible person. How dare you not think of me and tell me your deepest, darkest secret the first time we met and fell in love at the climbing wall."

I shook my head and laughed at his sarcasm.

"I get it."

I felt a presence behind me, and I turned to see Lisa standing there. Seriously? What nightmare was I in?

She glared so deeply at me, I had to break eye contact with her.

She raised her eyes. "Tim," she said with a nod.

He nodded back, his eyebrows scrunched up at the obvious tension between Lisa and me.

"I thought you were having Brad over for dinner," I said, unable to hide my relief. Maybe he stood her up after finally realizing she was a manipulative woman who was obviously trying to punish me by chasing my man. Not really my man at the moment. Or ever again, but still.

"For your information, it started to rain so we decided to go out for dinner. Of all the places we could pick, we just had to choose the place where the two of you would be on a date. I should have seen this coming."

I stood up now. "Excuse me? Brad is ... here? With you?"

It hurt like a knife being jammed into my chest and suddenly all the air left my lungs like a popped balloon. They were at this same restaurant on a date, together? I did not want to see this. I would never be able to unsee this. He was going to be so mad I was here with Tim. I looked behind her, but there was no sign of him.

"Yes, he's parking the car. Like a gentleman, he dropped me off at the door." She looked at Tim again. "So sad she let the man go, huh? She never deserved him."

Tim looked at me. "Maybe we should go?"

Before I could even think, Brad walked in the door with a smile on his face. Until he saw me and Tim. His smile turned upside down. He cleared his throat and made his way to his date. His date? This day could not get any worse.

"Tim, Madeline."

He used my full name. He was pissed, but was he more angry than I was?

He put his hand behind his neck. He looked terribly uncomfortable, but weren't we all?

Tim stood up to shake his hand. "Want to step outside with me for a second? Give the women some time to chat?"

Oh, please, no. I was not sure if I was angrier that they were going to leave me alone with my arch nemesis or that they were going outside to argue. What if it led to another physical fight? I really screwed up this time.

Tim followed behind Brad as he led the way outside. Lisa plopped down in the chair next to me. Why didn't I drive my car so I could get away fast? My house was not too far from here ...

"Just like it was ten years ago when you stole him from me."

Her words caught me off guard. "Excuse me?"

"You aren't even that cute. What do men see in you anyway? I just don't get it. You were such a dork in high school."

"I didn't steal Brad from you, Lisa. The two of you never even dated."

"Bullshit!"

The restaurant went quiet and everyone looked our way.

I forced a smiled at all the onlookers. "Just calm down. Let's talk about this like adults. You're making a scene."

She stomped her foot like a spoiled child, and her tone got even louder. "Adults? I'm making a scene? Brad and I were best friends until you showed up and stole him away from me. We would probably still be together if you hadn't gotten between us."

"Lisa, you were never together. Brad told me the two of you were never more than just friends. Do you really think you dated?"

She crossed her arms but did not answer my question. Instead, she said, "In high school we were best friends. Do you even remember that?"

I nodded, unsure where she was going with this. "Of course I do."

"Brad was a senior, and we were juniors. We would pass

him in the halls and he always said hello to you, even though I was the one who said hello to him. He was the big basketball player and we were nobody's. You were homely with those braces and glasses. But for some reason, everyone thought you were cool. But you weren't. I was cool. I was pretty. My dad was the mayor of Hibbing for christ's sake."

I just listened to her go on, along with everyone else at the restaurant.

"You never gave him any attention. You were too cool for me, for him, for everyone," she said, her voice rising again. "I was always in love with Brad. He finally started hanging out with me. We were on a volleyball league together for two years before you showed up. We took second place together. I even took private golf lessons so I could ask him to shoot golf balls with me after the volleyball season was over."

I listened to her speak. I knew she crushed on Brad, but he assured me they were never together and nothing had ever happened between them.

"Then you came along and got hired at the school as the librarian, once again getting in the way. He's my soul mate, you know? You treated him like crap and dumped him when the going got tough."

Enough of her revisionist history. I was putting an end to this nonsense. "I asked you if you had a crush on him and you said no, remember? You gave me your blessing, but ever since, you've had it out for me. Hell, you texted him after we were married, after we had a kid together. You texted him as soon as we split up. I don't understand why you would do this to a married man."

She stared me in the eyes, leaning forward on the table, a challenging look in her eyes.

"If he hadn't been with you, none of this would have happened. If you spent more time with your family instead of fussing over the birthday party, your daughter would still be alive. I was going to surprise Brad and Ariel by beating them to the museum that day, but I got a flat tire. He stopped to help me because that is the kind of guy he is, and then that car hit his car with Ariel inside. I was the one who was there and do you know what? I was ready to let him go after that, but you just threw him away like nothing."

"Excuse me? You were the reason they stopped the car on the side of the road? You're the reason that—I can't do this anymore. Stay away from me. Don't ever talk to me again. You're manipulative and evil and … and … crazy!"

I needed to get out fast, before I hit her or did something else she had coming to her. I grabbed my purse and jacket and ran out the door.

I heard her calling my name behind me. "Madeline, go ahead and run. It's what you're good at. Funny, you never seem to get anywhere though do you?"

I was in the parking lot when I realized I didn't drive, Tim did. I looked over at Brad and locked eyes with him, then I kept walking in the direction of my house.

She yelled after me. "I love him! Just let him go."

It took everything I had not to run at her and tackle her to the ground with a body slam or even a slap across her face with all my weight behind it.

"I was the one there for him. Where the hell were you?"

I threw my purse down on the ground and ran as fast as I could in her direction. Everyone has their breaking point and this was mine. She pushed me too far this time.

23

S he came flying at Lisa, surprising both him and Tim. In all the years he had been with his wife, he never saw her hit someone. She had Lisa straddled beneath her legs on the ground, punching her in the face when he finally pulled her off. Lisa had scratches and red marks all over her face, and Maddy had the angriest look in her eyes. He struggled to hold onto her arms as she tried to jump back on top of Lisa. Tim safeguarded Lisa behind him.

The struggle finally ended, and Maddy fell into his shoulder, crying. He turned her around and led her down the street, holding on to her arm to steady her. She no longer fought him, but let him lead her.

"What the hell happened between the two of you?"

She laughed through her tears, sniffling before she answered. "I'm sorry, but you have no idea how good that felt. She deserved it."

He just looked down, unsure of what to say.

"Brad, I need you to tell me exactly what happened that day. I've avoided this long enough."

. . .

THEY STOPPED on the side of the road, and he turned toward her. He used his thumb to wipe away a black streak under her eye. He had waited so long for this moment, to get everything off his chest but now that she was finally letting him, he worried she might never talk to him again once she heard it all.

"Ariel and I were passing Nashwauk when I got the text from Lisa. She said she wanted to surprise us at the museum for Ariel's birthday, but her car broke down a couple miles behind us. We turned around and went back to help her. When I parked on the shoulder of the highway, I told Ariel to wait in the car." He stopped to hold back the tears, the memories of that day so clear in his mind.

"I don't understand why you went back to help her. Why she thought she could just show up at a kid's birthday party she wasn't even invited to."

He ran a nervous hand through his hair and looked away so he wouldn't break down. "I'm not sure. It surprised me as well. I should have told you about her being there a long time ago. The problem is Lisa was going through some … stuff and she came to me, and I promised her I would keep her secret."

She crossed her arms in front. "You had secrets with Lisa?"

"No, no, no. It's not like that. Okay, Lisa had cancer, breast cancer. She was going through chemo. I was her boss and she told me in confidentiality. Well, I was the assistant principal, but still her boss. I wasn't supposed to tell anyone. I knew she was weak, and I couldn't help but support her. She didn't tell anyone else. She didn't want anyone to treat her any different."

"How do you know she wasn't lying?"

He stared at her. How many times had he asked himself this question and then felt terrible for even thinking it? He hung his head. "I don't. I wanted to believe she wouldn't lie."

"BRAD, she has all of her hair. She hasn't lost any weight. She never misses a day of school. She didn't back then either."

"I'm such an idiot."

"Tell me the rest. What happened after you stopped?"

"I got out of the car and went to check on her car, and she had a flat tire."

"At least she didn't lie about that."

He was an idiot for not telling her earlier. He didn't want her to relive this all over again. He didn't want to relive it all again either.

"There were two cars on the highway. One car speeded up to pass the other one but it was going too fast and hit our vehicle." He put his hands in front of his face. No longer could he hide the tears from her. He was supposed to be the strong one.

She cried with him, her hand on his back as he hunched over, hands on his knees, trying to catch his breath.

"It happened so fast. I tried to save her, Maddy, I promise. I tried so hard."

He looked up at her as she nodded, her eyes closed and the tears running more black streaks down her face.

She sobbed. "I know, I know. I never thought about how hard this must be for you. I swear I'm going to kill Lisa if she lied to you about the cancer."

"And what if we're wrong, and she did have cancer?"

"Well, I'm going to find out. But Brad, why did you bring her to dinner at the place where we got married?"

"I didn't think about it that way. I'm such an idiot."

"No, I believe you. I guess I'm just as guilty since I brought Tim there, too."

"I don't think she ever meant for anything to happen to Ariel. She's been there for me over the past few months, and you saw the way she acted after I cancelled the spring carnival. I needed to be on her good side so she wouldn't get me fired. You know how she can be."

"Brad, listen to yourself. That isn't a friend. She would take you aside and talk to you if she was a friend, and you wouldn't be second guessing whether or not she was lying to you about having cancer to get you to pay attention to her. Damn it, Brad, let her go. She isn't worth it."

"She doesn't really have friends. I just feel bad."

"She sucks, Brad. She isn't worth it. Tell me the truth, do you have any feelings at all for her?"

"Madeline, no, I love you, you know that. You mean the world to me. I wish I could take back the whole day Ariel died, but I can't. Lisa may be selfish and possibly a liar, but she would never want Ariel to get hurt."

"She tried to break up our marriage, you have to know that, but she isn't why our marriage fell apart." She wiped her tears with the back of her hand. "I may hate her, but I don't blame her for Ariel's death."

He looked at her and lifted her chin so her eyes met his. "I'm so sorry. You will always be the love of my life. No matter what. I want you to know that."

She smiled, still fighting her tears.

"I never had feelings for her, and I never meant to hurt you."

"I know."

They continued walking, now passing Pine Beach Resort. Campers were getting ready to spend the summer on the lake. The Pine Beach community was full of people who became families as they camped together all summer. They looked like they had no cares in the world, but isn't that the way we all try to make things seem?

"You are a good man, you know that?" she said, interrupting his thoughts.

"Thank you."

She nodded. "I need to have a conversation with Lisa after I cool off. Can we go somewhere for a little bit?"

"You hungry?"

"I am a little hungry."

He pointed behind them. "How about we walk back and have some pizza at Bimbos Octagon. I know how much you love their George's Special."

"You know banana peppers are my weakness," she said. She locked her arm in his and they turned around.

Bimbos was a family restaurant well known for its pizza and wings. A man name Bimbo started the restaurant and that became its name. The building was shaped in an octagon and was right off Side Lake, so in the summertime people docked their boats out front and ate inside or came by four wheeler after riding the trails all day.

THEY WERE SEATED at a table near the bar.

Maddy looked over her shoulder at the other customers. "It's not as busy tonight as I expected."

"Well, in the next week or two, it'll be hard to find a table."

"I haven't even asked. How's your dad doing?"

He was not sure what to say. How honest should he be? "Not that well."

"Oh no. What's going on?"

"He's having a hard time breathing, and he's really struggling cognitively."

She sat there in shock. Her eyes glossed over. He wanted to hold her in his arms again, but he was numb from it all.

"I am so sorry," she finally said. "I guess you haven't been able to see him then?"

187

"I got to see him for a little bit last night. He's in and out. Half the time it's as if he doesn't even know who he is."

Madeline placed her hand on his, giving him goosebumps at her touch. He smiled and squeezed her hand back.

"Is there anything I can do?"

He shook his head. "There isn't much any of us can do. Just pray, I guess."

He checked his phone for the hundredth time this evening. Still nothing from his mother, which he suspected was good.

"How are your mom and Lyndsey holding up? They must be heartbroken."

"They're doing as well as expected. I'm going to stop by my mom's after dinner here. Check on her. They have been sending her home at night, and I think it is because she needs her rest more than it is for him."

"Your mother is so kind to be there for him. It can't be easy watching someone you love go through something like that." Maddy said. She nervously twirled her hair when she realized she was pretty much describing them.

They ate dinner without much conversation because they were both hungry.

After they finished eating, Brad took the tab to the bar and came back.

"I guess we probably need to walk back to Riverside and get your car, huh?"

"Oh yeah, I forgot I left it there."

He held the door open for her, and they walked back to the restaurant.

I kept thinking about Brad's father. "I can't believe it. Do they think he will get his memory back?"

"The doctor seems to think so."

"Is there anything I can do?"

"Why don't you come over to my parent's house with me? Lyndsey and my mom would love to see you."

She hesitated, then nodded. "Okay."

"MOM, are you here? It's Brad and Maddy is here, too."

His mother came running out with swollen eyes and red blotches all over her face. She wrapped her arms around Maddy and looked like she would never let go. They both cried in each other's arms, and he had to step away. So many damn memories, and he could only imagine how hard this was for Maddy to face. They lost their daughter, and now Maddy had to go through another loss. She was always so close to his father, he was like a father to her. They were always joking around and ganging up on him. Although it drove him crazy at the time, that was the kind of bond she had with his father. His whole family lost Ariel and then Maddy after the accident.

He had changed since his world was torn upside down. Losing Ariel changed everything.

"I'm so glad you came back. I wasn't really myself when I saw you at the hospital," his mother said. "It's been a really hard couple of weeks."

Maddy smiled through the tears and wiped her eyes. "I can only imagine. I'm sorry for everything you have been going through. I just wish there was more I could do to help."

The stairs creaked behind him. Lyndsey ran toward Maddy and their mother. "I thought I heard your voice."

He loved watching the most important women in his life together again.

"How are you?" Maddy said to Lyndsey.

"Better now. I'm glad you came over." Lyndsey turned to Brad and winked at him.

His sister wanted them back together almost as much as he did.

"I'm so sorry about your dad. Any updates?"

Lyndsey shook her head.

"I'm so sorry," Madeline said.

"Enough about that or I'm going to end up crying again. What's new with you? How are you? You look amazing by the way," Brad's mom said with an arm around Maddy's shoulder.

"You just saw her a couple days ago," Lyndsey said.

"I know, but I was in shock, and I never got a chance to talk to her."

"It has been a very difficult time for us lately, hasn't it?" Madeline paused. "We have all been through so much, but I'm back to work anyway."

They made their way into the kitchen, leaving Brad confused and unsure of whether or not he should follow. His mother paused and turned around to face him. "Are you coming?"

He shrugged his shoulders. "I don't know. Maybe you guys need some girl time. I may take a nap. Wake me up when Maddy's ready to leave, and I'll walk her home."

"Bradley."

"Yeah?"

"Don't quit fighting for her." With that she turned and walked into the kitchen.

He made his way upstairs and opened his blinds to gaze over the lake. He would never quit fighting for her. He was lost without her.

She meant everything to him and maybe, just maybe, she was falling back in love with him, too. He could only hope.

24

W e talked for a couple hours, then sat in the living room and watched a movie.

Everyone went to bed after the movie was over. I tiptoed upstairs to say goodbye to Brad with his mom's insistence before I walked home. His door was ajar, so I knocked lightly. The light shone on him from the hallway behind me. His shirt was off and the sheets pulled down. I stared at his chest. Memories of when we made love a few days ago, like it was for the first time, flashed through my mind.

He was in so much pain with everything going on, and what a jerk I was to make it all about me this past year. Just because he had a hard time talking about his emotions did not mean he was fine. I slowly shut the door, careful not to wake him.

I turned around to find Lyndsey standing there.

"You can wake him up, he won't mind."

I thought about it. "No, he looks so sweet. I'll let him sleep."

"You two really made one hell of a couple, you know that?"

I nodded. I did not want to talk about this right now, maybe never.

"I don't mean to pry," she said. "You guys have always been my relationship goals. The love the two of you shared was that once-in-a-lifetime kind of love. He misses you."

"I miss that, too, but it will never be the same."

"I see the way you look at him. I wouldn't be me if I didn't say something. Let him love you. I know the two of you can make it through this. He needs you now more than ever."

His bedroom door creaked open. I stared into his eyes, my body suddenly overheating.

"Are you heading home? I didn't expect to sleep this long."

Lyndsey opened her bedroom door. "Goodnight."

Maddy yawned. "Yeah, I'm on my way home. Just thought I'd say goodbye."

"Let me walk you."

I thought about fighting him for a split second, but changed my mind as Lyndsey's words repeated in my head. "Okay."

THE NIGHT WAS BEAUTIFUL. The air was warm for this time of year, and the outside light turned on as we walked past it.

"I miss running with you in the morning. Maybe we could start doing that every morning again?"

He smiled. "I would love that."

"Are you still running in the mornings without me?"

"Yes. It helps clear my head."

We walked in silence. The crickets in the distance were hypnotizing. As we made our way into my yard, I turned to him. "Want to walk out to the dock with me and put our feet in the water like we always used to?"

"I'd love that."

We took off our shoes, and I was the first to put my feet in. I pulled them out immediately. The coldness of the water made my whole body shiver.

"Cold?"

Before I could answer, his feet were in the water. "It feels nice."

I giggled and nudged him playfully. "You would say that."

"No, really. Take a deep breath and let it out as you put your feet in. Just like you did in the ice bath, remember?"

I did as he said, and this time I did not pull them out. I was still pretty chilled, but it was nowhere near as bad as the ice bath.

"Do you ever wonder what would have happened if Ariel was still alive?"

"All the time," he said.

I turned to him, and he lifted his head to look at me. "Do you think we would still be together?"

He pushed a strand of hair behind my ear, and his hand lingered there for a moment. "Without a doubt."

"Do you regret the other night?"

His eyebrows lifted. "Not one bit. Do you?"

I looked down at my lap. "I was worried it would complicate things between us."

He laced his hand in mine and kissed it.

"Do you remember that time Ariel was at your mom's house playing hide-and-seek and we couldn't find her? We ran around the house looking everywhere and thought she must have run out the door?" I said.

"We were in a panic, weren't we? Then we found her in the clothes hamper, of all places."

I laughed at the vivid memory.

"The way she giggled when you opened it up. She had to be the quietest four-year-old when she hid."

"Do you remember her dance programs? She was only three, but every little girl in the class watched her so they could follow. She was such a leader."

"I can't believe she's gone. Sometimes I feel like I don't have a purpose anymore without her. She was too young to be taken from us."

I got teary eyed and he pulled my head onto his shoulder. "I may not show it, and I know that frustrates you, but my heart is broken. I am so sorry I wasn't able to protect her. I'll never forgive myself for that, you know."

I PULLED MY HEAD BACK. "I hope you understand why I need to confront Lisa."

"Just hear her out, okay? Maybe she wasn't lying about the cancer. I'd like to think not."

"I'm sorry I didn't listen before. I just needed some time."

"I know."

"I still can't believe she was stalking you like that. She is a terrible person. I can't believe I was ever friends with her."

"I know."

"I knew you guys were having your little bon-fire at her house, and I was upset but glad I wouldn't have to see it. But when you showed up at Riverside with her, I was so angry and so hurt."

He looked away. "I know, because that was the way I felt when I walked in your classroom door and there you were kissing Tim. I've never been in a fight before."

I laughed at the memory of it. "I don't think I would consider that a fight. I'd call it more of a swing and miss."

He covered his face with his hand. "He laid me out flat, that's for sure. I'll give him that. I never was really the fighting type."

"For you to try to hit someone because you were jealous actually turned me on a little bit."

"Really? It did? That was probably the most embarrassing thing I've ever done. Not my proudest moment."

"But if you ever try to hit someone in a school again, I won't be as understanding."

"I know. None of the teachers would be. I still can't believe he told everyone we staged the whole fight scene. No one actually believed it, did they?"

"I think Lisa did, but that's not saying much."

"You really hate her, don't you?"

"She chased you for how long and lied to you about having cancer. She also really believes the two of you had this fictional relationship. She is messed up."

He put his hand on mine. "She must have a pretty bad life to be that angry and manipulative. She can't feel very good about herself."

"Still. She can't get away with that, no matter how bad her life is. It's horrible."

"Just make sure when you do talk to her, you keep an open mind, okay?"

I let out a loud, angry groan. "Why do you keep protecting her? You know she's lying just as much as I do. She played you, and you keep feeding into it. I don't know why I thought you had changed. Whatever this is or was, it's over. "

I couldn't stop myself as the words poured out. My whole body burned with fire. Why was he protecting her? I hated the part of me that felt so insecure. I couldn't think straight until I confronted her. I needed to know the truth. I didn't care how late it was. I would find my answers.

25

I went straight to Lisa's house to confront her, but no one answered the door. I went around to the back and found her on the deck in her hot tub enjoying a glass of red wine.

She sat up tall when she saw me, obviously caught off-guard.

"Are you here to attack me? Because if you are, I'm calling the police." She stood up in her hot tub and started to climb over the edge.

"I'm not here to assault you, Lisa, even though you deserve it for lying to everyone."

"What are you talking about? I told you the truth about the day Ariel died. You just feel guilty for not being with your family when it happened."

"I'm here because I need to know the truth," I said. "No more lies."

"I have told you everything. I'm not backing away from Brad. I know he loves me, too. He is just so blinded by you for some reason. Poor guy. You could do everyone a favor and disappear. Don't you think you've hurt him enough?"

"How dare you chase my husband? Shame on you. You know nothing about my relationship with Brad." My hands were shaking so I placed them behind my back to hide them from her. "I'm here because you told Brad you had cancer, and that was why he answered your texts and couldn't be mean to you while you were trying to break up our marriage."

She cleared her throat and took a sip of wine. "I don't know what you're talking about." She couldn't even look me in the eye anymore.

"You came to him knowing he was moving into the principal role and told him you were going through cancer because you knew he couldn't tell anyone. You made him promise. You had it all planned out, didn't you? Make him feel sorry for you, tell him the cancer was gone. Get him to fall in love with you. Why would he ever suspect you lied about it, right?"

"Get out of my house."

I looked around me. "I'm not in your house, Lisa. We're outside. The problem was, he didn't love you because he was in love with his WIFE!"

"You're still on private property, don't make me call the police."

"Go ahead. You want me to leave? Just answer my question. Were you or were you not lying when you told Brad you had cancer?"

She stood up in the hot tub again, this time reaching for her towel and wrapping it around her body. She took a step toward her back door, but I jumped in front of her.

"Oh no, you don't. I need to know the truth."

"You want to know the truth?"

I crossed my arms in front of my body to keep them from hitting her.

"I told him I had cancer to try to save him from you."

I shook my head. "How would that save him from me exactly?"

"You were toxic, and he deserved to be with someone who loved him."

I turned around. "That is all I needed to hear. You are sick, you know that? You know nothing about my relationship with Brad. Who are you to judge? Get your own damn relationship and maybe next time go for a man who is single and actually likes you back."

She ran around in front of me, almost losing her towel. "I hate you! I don't understand how he can still want you. After everything you've done to him!"

I COULD NOT HIDE my shock. "He was my husband," I said through clenched teeth. "That was really low, even for you."

She turned away from me and it took everything in me not to tackle her after she added, "He would be with me if that car hadn't killed Ariel."

I held my breath and reminded myself I needed to walk away, but I couldn't get my feet to move. We stood there in silence, shooting evil daggers at each other.

"I feel so sorry for you," I said. "You're delusional. Oh, and by the way, I slept with him two days ago, and it was the best sex we have EVER had. Too bad he will never touch you that way, huh?"

That was a low blow, but it was that or hit her and without Brad or Tim to hold me back, I wasn't sure I would be able to stop punching her once I started. That was not me at all, but she brought out the worst in me. Desperate times call for desperate measures, I guess.

She stared at me without a word. I took this as my cue and turned to leave. "Enjoy your night alone with all your friends."

"I will," she said, her voice more of a scream. "Enjoy going home to your empty house because you and I both know you may be screwing Brad, but you will never be strong enough to forgive him and be with him again. You only care about yourself. Let him go so he can be happy. You never will though, will you? You'll just keep him in misery for the rest of his life. He's never going to be good enough for you, is he?"

A door slammed. I glanced over my shoulder to make sure she had disappeared behind it. I had the answer I was looking for so why did I feel so awful? The truth would hurt Brad, and that was the last thing I wanted. I did want him to be happy, I did.

26

The spring carnival and the last day of school arrived. Brad was glad to have three months off, but was sad he would not be seeing Maddy every day at school anymore. Sure, she lived just a couple doors down and they were still friends, but she was the highlight of his day, every day. He worried she would move on, and he would be left living with his parents for the rest of his life. He felt bad even thinking that, considering his father's health.

He arrived at the school a little before six in the morning to make sure set up was going well, and the bouncy houses were blown up on time. The air was a bit chilly, but would become hot and sunny later, with no rain in the forecast.

The cotton candy machine and snow cone maker were set up in tents, and the dunk tank was in the parking lot. The volunteers started arriving at seven-thirty, and his nerves began to calm. Bowling and fishing games were set up outside, and they had a magician, face painting, and a couple of mom's dressed as Disney princesses.

· · ·

HE WENT into his office and put on his Superman costume, along with the red cape Madeline got him to wear on Halloween a few years ago. He would probably overheat out in the sun all day, but it was worth it because the looks on the children's faces brought a smile to his face.

Madeline always volunteered to be in charge of the carnival throughout the day, and he was glad to help this year and be able to spend more time with her.

She was at the cotton candy machine under the tent with a parent, showing her how to use the machine when he walked out. She was dressed in her Supergirl costume, which made his heart flutter.

He did not realize he was staring until their eyes locked, and her face turned red. He turned away and went to check on the plug-ins for the bouncy houses before the first group of kindergartners came out.

When he returned, Tim was standing next to Madeline as she announced instructions to both classes. After she sent the kids to play, she chatted with Tim again. They laughed and pointed at the kids. Would he ever be okay with her being with someone else?

He could not get caught staring at them so he made his way over to the line of kids waiting for cotton candy and snow cones. The volunteers gave out the treats to the children and did not seem to need any help so he moved on to the bouncy house. He needed to keep his mind busy.

He had to redirect the children a few times due to a couple aggressive kids, but overall they were laughing and having a good time. He smiled at the thought of his daughter. Ariel loved the bouncy houses. Maddy took her to the spring carnival every year since she was little. She listened so well when Maddy told her what to do to help, from opening the white paper bags for popcorn to testing out the bouncy houses to make sure everything looked good. He smiled at the memories as if they were yesterday.

He turned around to glance at her and Tim, but instead he saw Tim headed in his direction.

"Hey," Tim said. He put out his hand to shake and stood next to him as they watched the children jumping in the bouncy house.

"How's it going?"

"Pretty good. What a great day it turned out to be. The kids are sure having a good time. Maddy tells me you put most of this together. I would have never known after your speech that day," Tim said with an unreadable expression.

Tim's hands were crossed in front of him as he waved back at some kids jumping inside the long caterpillar bouncy house.

Brad wiped the sweat off the back of his neck. "Yeah, that wasn't one of my best days."

"I know. I also know you lost it because you saw Maddy and me kissing." He paused.

Brad turned to look at him. What the hell was he trying to do? And today of all days?

"I'm sorry about that. Maddy is an amazing person and had you not been her ex-husband and father of her child, I would have fought harder."

Was this his way of apologizing?

Tim turned toward him now. "What I'm trying to say is there is no competition. I know she loves you, and I'm not here to challenge that. I think the two of you have had enough of people trying to get in the middle of your relationship."

"What do you mean?"

"I was there that day at Riverside, remember? When Maddy practically pummeled Lisa," Tim said with a laugh. "If you and I hadn't been there to hold her back, who knows what would have happened. I was surprised when Maddy went to Lisa that night all by herself and didn't beat the crap out of her. Am I right?"

He stared at Tim blankly. "What do you mean went to Lisa's? Maddy never told me she went to Lisa's that night. She said she decided not to."

Tim ran a nervous hand through his hair. "Oh man, I'm sorry. I didn't know. I thought—"

"Tim, tell me what happened. You owe me that."

He put his hands up. "I don't really know, man. Don't shoot the messenger. She literally just told me about it like two minutes ago. I don't think it's a secret, she probably just didn't get around to telling you yet. I don't want to start any problems. I came over here with hopes of us starting over. I didn't mean to upset you."

"What do you know?" he said, challenging Tim.

Tim looked behind him, making sure Maddy was nowhere near them.

"I'm not sure why she didn't tell you, but she went to Lisa's that night, and Lisa admitted she never had cancer. It was all a lie to get you to feel sorry for her."

He couldn't believe it. Maddy was so sure Lisa lied and told him she was going to get the truth. Why didn't she tell him? He felt like a fool. Why did Tim know the truth but not him?

"Man, I'm sorry. I'm not sure why she didn't tell you, but I'm sure she has a good reason. I know she loves you."

He stood there, trying to figure it out himself.

"I really don't want to start problems. I was trying to apologize so I'm sorry if I stirred up any trouble."

"Then why did you come over here? The last time we talked, you told me you were pretty much fighting for my girl."

"Yeah, I feel terrible about that. That was before I knew

about Ariel and everything. I want you to know she may be in a bad place right now, but she definitely loves you. I really hope the two of you can get past all that. I also want to let you know I've been offered a full-time teaching job at the high school here in Hibbing."

Brad stared at him in silence for a minute.

Tim looked a little nervous so Brad patted his back.

"Sorry if I came off like a jerk, you just surprised me, that's all. Seriously, congratulations. It takes a real man to come over to me and apologize. You may have caught me off guard a little bit, but I do believe you mean well. I'm not going to lie, I am glad you aren't working at my school anymore."

Tim laughed and shook Brad's hand. "I understand, sir. I'm sorry we got off on the wrong foot, but I want you to know I respect you and I won't be a problem." Tim glanced at his watch and turned to walk away.

"Wait, Tim ..." Brad said.

"Yeah?"

"I want to say thank you."

"For what?"

"For being there for her when I couldn't. For being her friend."

He smiled and nodded. "She made it easy. You're one lucky man."

"One last question."

Tim turned around.

Brad wasn't sure how to ask so he just stood there trying to find the right words.

"No, we never slept together," he said and walked away.

How the hell did Tim know that was exactly what he couldn't find the words to ask?

. . .

BRAD SEARCHED the crowd for Maddy, but she was nowhere to be seen. The first group of second graders would not arrive for twenty minutes. Just enough time to take a quick break from the sun and get a drink of water while he processed the information Tim gave him. He believed Tim was sorry and that he didn't know Maddy hadn't told him about going to Lisa's. The only thing he didn't understand was why she lied to him. Why she wouldn't tell him.

He leaned his head over the water fountain and heard a foot tapping behind him. He stood up and turned around.

"You sure take forever," Maddy said with a smirk.

He wiped his face and waited for her to take a drink. "Don't stomp your little last season Prada shoes at me, honey," he said with a smirk.

He watched as her eyes opened wide and she started laughing so hard, she had to bend over.

"Legally Blonde! You remembered!"

"Well, yeah, you had me watch that movie how many times?"

"You just made my whole day," she said, still laughing. "I'm sorry, but that was amazing."

They walked down the hall together, and the smile did not leave her face.

Once they were in front of his office, her expression became serious. "Can I talk to you for a minute?"

"Of course, why don't we go into my office?"

Maddy shut the door behind her. "I need to get back outside, but this will only take a minute."

"Okay?"

"I want you to hear this from me. I applied as the head librarian at the public library, and I have an interview tomorrow." She stared at him, a nervous look on her face as she waited for his reaction.

He swallowed the lump in his throat and cleared his

throat before speaking. "I thought things were going better now. Are you looking for another job? Is it something I did?"

"No, not at all. You know it's always been my dream, and I promised myself I wouldn't make any big changes for one year after Ariel passed away. The year is almost up."

His stomach tightened. He selfishly wanted her to stay here, with him. He wanted to scream, *Don't go!* But she deserved better, and this was what she wanted.

"Thank you for telling me. I do have a question for you though."

Her smile dropped. "What's that?"

"Why didn't you tell me you went to Lisa's house after you left my parents?"

She turned around and faced the window, her back to him. "Ugh."

"Why didn't you tell me she admitted that she never had cancer?"

She turned back around, her face white. "I'm sorry I lied. I didn't want to hurt you. You trusted her."

He grabbed her hips. "I'm not mad at you, but I didn't expect to hear it from Tim first."

"I'm so sorry. I never should have told him. That night was pretty horrible, but I'm glad I finally found out the whole truth about that day. I'm sorry it took me so long to talk to you about that night. I wasn't ready to hear it until now."

"I should have told you about Lisa. As your husband, I never should have kept that from you. You would have seen right through her, and I was a fool."

SHE LOOKED SURPRISED. "It hurt that you didn't tell me, but I know I pushed you away and never gave you a chance to tell me about it all. I'm sorry for what I put you through." She touched his forearm, and his heart screamed inside him. "Friends?"

No, he wanted to be more than friends. Why did everyone say she loved him still? Tim was wrong, she did not love him. She was never going to forgive him.

"Friends," he said, not meaning it at all.

"Well, I'd better get back to the carnival."

He had a hard time smiling after that. Lisa led her class outside, and Madeline gave her speech to the kids about being considerate, taking turns, and listening to the teacher when the whistle blew. As the kids all ran off, Lisa approached him.

He had a hard time looking at her after finding out the truth of her manipulation. She played him for a fool.

"Madeline gave me a little visit the other day."

"So I heard."

"I almost called the police."

He bit his lip to stop from saying anything too unprofessional. He was, in fact, her boss.

"It's all about her all the time. Did you tell her about us?"

"Us?"

"You know, that we were a thing before the two of you hooked up."

"I'm sorry, Lisa, but we were not a thing." Why did she keep pushing her delusions? This could go in the wrong direction fast.

"I know she pushed for the relationship, but you and I have always had a connection. If it wasn't for her, we would be together."

He turned to her. "Lisa, why would you ever want to be someone's second best, first of all? And secondly, you were my friend, nothing more. If I gave you the impression it was more, I am sorry."

She put her hands on her hips, and her expression turned

hard. "How does she still have control over you after you divorced? She's cold, don't you know that by now? I never would have done that to you. Don't you see that? Stop wasting your time on her. She's never cared about anyone but herself."

His jaw clenched. "Now, that's my daughter's mother you're talking about. You need to stop."

"Don't tell me you think this is my fault."

He rubbed his temple with two fingers, wishing her and his headache away. He wanted to confront her about her lies, but this was not the time.

"You aren't thinking clearly. She has you so wrapped around her damn finger. Don't you see? It's been me all this time. I would treat you well. No games."

She wrapped her hands around his arm before he had a chance to react.

In one quick motion, he shrugged her off. "Go for a walk. I have taken your crap for far too long."

"That's not true," she said. "Tell me you don't really think that. She's manipulating you again, isn't she?"

She had no idea, and it was time for him to finally tell her. Even if he lost his job over this, it must be said. "I've tried so hard to be nice to you. You kept texting and calling and step-ping over the line since ... well, since I first got into a rela-tionship with Maddy. You continued to text me at inappropriate times. And you followed me. You told me you had cancer and you lied. What about the chemo? Radiation? It was all lies so what, you thought I would just leave my wife for you? Well, you thought wrong. I don't love you, Lisa, and I never will."

Her mouth hung open. She closed it and lessened the gap between them until she was right in his face, her finger pointed so close to his eye, he wondered if she was going to poke him with it.

"You listen here, buddy. I saw the looks you gave me. You encouraged the attention. I knew once you knocked her up, it was a long shot between us. I waited because I knew you would get bored with her fast. I made up the cancer story to help you. How do you not see that? She had you under her spell, and you needed a little push."

He covered her finger with his hand and stepped back. "It is never going to happen. Never ever. You are a liar and a manipulator. I can't believe I felt bad for you."

"But--"

"You and I are never going to happen. NEVER EVER," he repeated. "Do I make myself clear?"

She shook her head, then nodded. "I quit."

At first, he did not think he heard her right.

"What?"

She cleared her throat. "I quit. I'm out of here. Just don't forget I warned you about her. If you want to keep taking her crap, you go ahead."

He watched her storm past the tent and back into the building, and he slowly followed behind to see where exactly she was going. She was angry, and he was technically still responsible for her. Was she leaving right now in the middle of the day? Surely she would finish her day or at least clear out her classroom. She continued to walk down the sidewalk.

"Where are you going, teacher?" little Tommy Stewart said

She turned around, took two steps in his direction, and said, "I no longer work here. I'm sure Miss Jones will have no problem filling in."

She walked right past Maddy and let out a loud grunt as she continued walking right past her.

Maddy looked at her with a confused expression and then looked to Brad for answers.

"What happened?" she mouthed.

"Goodbye, whore," Lisa said over her shoulder as she walked straight to her car.

Maddy placed her hands over little Tommy's ears and gasped.

"What's a whore, teacher?" he said with a confused look.

She shook her head and so did Brad, but they continued watching Lisa.

Lisa pulled on the door handle of her car and jiggled it. She did not have her purse or her keys. She threw up her hands and stomped her way inside once she realized she wasn't going to get very far.

He followed behind her to her classroom. Moments like this, he wished he was not the principal and could just stay out of it.

"Principal Jones," Tommy Stewart said.

Brad stopped. "Yes, Tommy."

"Is she really gone forever?"

He kneeled down in front of him.

"Yes, but don't worry, it's the last day of school and you will have a different teacher next year."

"I know. I'm so glad she's gone because I was worried about all the first graders who would have her as a teacher next year. She's evil."

"You are? She is?"

He had no idea the kids did not like her. Sure, she was mean to the adults, but he thought she was a good teacher. She sure put on a show and had them all believing she liked children.

Tommy tugged on Brad's shirt. "One more thing."

"Yes," Brad said standing back up.

"Do you think Mrs. Jones would tell us some more jokes? She's really funny."

"She is?"

He glanced at Maddy, and she looked shocked.

"She is," he said before he ran off to get some more candy.

ONCE LISA WAS GONE for good, Brad got into the dunk tank and spent a half hour as kids tried to hit the target with a softball.

The second graders went in for lunch and out came the first graders. They tried dunking him, but their aim was not on. He was sweating while sitting on the seat of the dunk tank, but the water was ice cold beneath his feet. He watched Maddy whisper something into Brittany's ear after three missed attempts at hitting the button. Brittany dropped the last softball and came running at the button full speed and pushed it with her hand.

The cold water took the air out of his lungs, and he quickly surfaced to find the ladder and climb out.

Maddy stood there smiling at him. "Take deep breaths and try not to focus on how cold the water is, Principal Jones," she said.

"I wouldn't laugh. You're next." He splashed her with water as he exited. She was finally letting herself laugh and joke and not be so serious all the time. She was quick-witted and he loved that about her. He never thought he would fall more in love with her, but he was more and more every day. If only she felt the same way.

It felt like any other day. The sun was shining, the birds were singing, the grass was green, and the sky was so blue. I walked the trail, which was now lined with lilies and marigolds, and stopped to smell buds on a rose bush. The secret forest had always been beautiful, but it was as if I was seeing it for the first time in a new light.

I reached the pond and there he was sitting on our bench. He got up and looked at me. A smile spread across his face. "I've been waiting for you."

"You have?"

I knew he would be here today. The pond was our daughter's favorite place when she was alive, and the place Brad and I shared as we fell in love, and we thought our love would last forever. I shivered at the thought.

"I have."

He put out his hand, and I placed mine in his. He guided me around the pond and into the trees, pulling back branches for me until we reached a giant rock where he sat down and patted the space next to him.

I sat down. His expression was full of sadness but also what looked like hope.

"I've been doing a lot of research on butterflies and how to plant butterfly gardens. I planted milkweeds to attract the monarch caterpillars. They flower in purple, pink, yellow, orange, and white."

I looked at the thick stalks of green plants around me. "Ariel would have loved this. What a great way to keep her spirit alive."

He blushed and looked into my eyes with hope. "You don't think it's a little late?"

"It's never too late. Think of all the little kids who come here with their parents and chase the butterflies like Ariel did."

He took both my hands in his and turned toward me. "I miss our family, Madeline. I miss you."

I found it hard to believe a man with such a strong jawline and thick arms was able to express so much emotion. Instead of wiping away his tears, I rested my head on his shoulder. He pulled me in and squeezed me."

"I miss you," I whispered.

He pushed my hair back behind my shoulder. "I miss you, too."

I pulled my head away after a few moments and looked at the beautiful oak trees before us. "Maybe we could go for a run later and then you can grill some venison burgers. I still have all that meat in the freezer from the deer you shot a couple years back."

"I would love that."

"I'm surprised your parents did not come," I said.

He held his breath. "Dad still isn't doing very well, and mom's health has been going downhill, too. Lyndsey moved in to help me take care of them, but it's only a matter of time before they go into a nursing home. Lyndsey works full time now as a social worker. She can't be there with them all the time, and it hasn't been easy. I do what I can, but I'm only around for the summer, and it's a lot for both of us."

"I can understand that. They were fine not too long ago. Life sure changes fast. Did she get that job in child protection she was hoping for?"

He nodded.

"I always admired her for what she does. Being a social worker can't be easy. I just wish she could find a good guy. I don't think she realizes what a catch she is."

"She's pretty great." He kissed the top of my head. "But so are you."

We went back to the pond, and he pulled out a pink and gold box from his pocket. He ran his fingers over the box and then handed it to me and I cried.

"How can our baby be in a box so small?"

Instead of answering me, he interlocked his fingers with mine and we rested our foreheads together with the urn in between our torsos.

"I THINK this is where she would want her ashes spread. It just hurts so bad to let them go."

"Our memories with Ariel will always be right here in our hearts and in the memories we keep. Let's do this together."

I opened the box and together we sprinkled the ashes in the air. The wind took them and blew them out of sight . The sun shone through the trees, and my heart filled with joy. He was right, her memory would always live inside us. I knew right then that Brad and I were always stronger together, I just never realized it before.

"Hey, Brad."

"Yeah."

I grabbed his hand. "Maybe after we barbecue, you could light up the campfire."

He squeezed my hand. "That sounds like a wonderful idea."

I took his face in my hands. "I never stopped loving you, boss."

He laughed and wrapped his hands around my waist as we kissed. It was a kiss I never wanted to end. I'm not sure if he pulled away or if it was me, but only because we both needed to breathe.

A butterfly flew between us as we parted, leaving us both with smiles because we knew she was right there with us. She always was.

I HEARD a knock at my door and there he stood, a box in hand. It was happening, he was here, back home, to stay. We unpacked his car, and I followed him into the bedroom as we both collapsed onto the bed with exhaustion. He lay there on his side, staring at me.

"What?"

Instead of answering me, his lips pressed against mine.

Our clothes came off fast and landed in a pile on the floor. We made love right there in our bed, but it was different this time because I knew this time it was forever.

I stared at his naked backside as he got out of bed. He had never been shy. He reached into a box and grabbed something in his hand. I sat up and wrapped the sheet around my naked body.

"What is that?"

He opened his hand and showed me the locket. I touched it and looked up at him again.

"Open it," he said.

I opened it up and cried at the pictures inside. "This is so beautiful," I said with tears in my eyes. I blinked them away and he leaned in to kiss me, then took it from my hand.

I lifted my hair as he secured it around my neck and then moved the locket so it was perfectly centered against my chest.

"Thank you. I love it."

"I love you," he said. "I know my grandmother would want you to have it. It is finally right where it belongs, around your neck."

WE STARTED SWIMMING in the lake in front of our house to get in shape for the triathlon. Of course, he was much faster than I was.

"It's so dark and hard to see in the water. Why is a pool so much easier to swim in?"

"It just takes practice," he said.

"Is it true people run you over in the water if you don't go fast enough in a triathlon?"

"As long as you don't start out in the front, I think you'll be fine. You're a strong swimmer, and I'll be right there to cheer you on. The women go first."

I was a little worried I would drown out there, but Brad convinced me there were lifeguards in kayaks who would be watching. What the hell would a guy in a kayak do to help me if I was drowning? I guess I would worry about that when the time came.

"How's Whitney doing by the way? Is she planning on joining us?"

"Her leg is still healing. The doctor said she will have no problem returning to work in the fall, but she can't complete any triathlons right now."

"Understandable. Did I tell you Lyndsey is coming to watch you, along with one of her best friends who used to live at the end of our road on Turtle Creek growing up? She lives in the cities but doesn't ever come to Side Lake because her and her mom had a falling out a while back."

"Oh, sad. What happened?"

"I'm not really sure. Her mom lives in the enormous house with the long driveway."

"The Johnson's house? Like the enormous mansion with the long driveway?"

"Yep."

"Wow. Well, I'd love to meet her too. I guess money doesn't buy happiness, huh? There must be a good reason why they don't talk but it's still sad. "

"Lyndsay said she can't wait to introduce you. You'd really like her."

I stared out into the lake that reminded me of all the wonderful times we had swimming with Ariel. For once the memory of her brought a smile to my face instead of a chest full of anxiety. There were just so many good times.

"What are you thinking about?"

My head shot in his direction. I wasn't sure how long I'd been staring off into space, thinking about it all. "How I'm going to swim to the dock and back faster than you."

He raised his eyebrow. "That sounds like a bet. Loser has to give the winner a back rub?"

"You're on," I said. I dove under the water before he could react.

Once he passed me and we swam to shore, I jumped on his back, and he splashed me.

"You're such a cheater, Mrs. Jones."

I kissed him. "Looks like I get a massage after all. I win."

He laughed back at me, and then he splashed water in my face.

O n a nice cool morning, I pushed my bike to the orange flags. No spectators were allowed in the flags where the bikes were lined up, and the athletes were getting prepared for the race.

Brad and I walked down to the beach to watch the boats set out the big orange balls that marked the swimming course.

"You swim around that orange circle and then around the other one, and then you come back and get out here," he said pointing.

I held my breath at the thought. "I'm pretty sure I'm going to die," I said. "Is it too late to get back in the car and go home?"

"You're not going to die. You've been training all summer for this. Plus, you have to follow Whitney's pink letters to happiness."

I laughed at his interpretation.

"Speaking of Whitney, have you seen her or your sister?"

He looked around. "No, I thought she was riding here with us."

"She was going to ride down with Lyndsey and Kat."

"Kat?"

"You know, the girl Lyndsey went to school with, the Johnson's daughter. Remember?"

"Oh, I didn't realize that was her name. I just got a text from her. They are around here somewhere."

The announcer began giving instructions to the participants. The women lined up in single file from the orange cone next to the water. A man pushed a button for each swimmer to start and they either ran or dove into the water.

I had a band with a GPS securely strapped around my ankle with Velcro for the organizers to time each participant. I stood about halfway down the line because I did not want to get stuck behind anyone slow, or get kicked in the face, or have someone run over me because I was too slow. I pulled my pink swim cap down over my hair.

Someone tapped me on the shoulder.

Another pink swim cap and big brown eyes stared back at me. She held out her hand for me to shake.

"You must be Madeline. I'm Katrina or Kat. Lyndsey pointed you out. I thought I'd introduce myself. It's my first time doing one of these triathlons and well, I'm a bit nervous I'm going to die."

"Me too. I'm so relieved to have someone to swim with."

I looked behind Kat and waved at Whitney and Lyndsey. They gave me a thumbs up, and I returned the gesture. I pushed my goggles on my eyes, and Kat did the same.

"You live in the cities, right?"

"Yeah, I'm a CPS social worker in Hennepin."

"Oh, child protection. It must be so hard. I always admired Lyndsey for what she does. I know it's pretty demanding work."

"It's definitely a stressful job. Hey look, everyone is getting in line."

I stepped back so she could go in front of me.

"You first," Kat said.

I TOOK off into the water after I heard the beep. Running in the water was hard work, but once I finally dove under, the water was lukewarm. I followed some kicking feet in front of me, and peeked in front of me every ten or so strokes. Every time I lifted my head I had veered left.

I had to pass the person in front of me since she was a bit slow. My hands grabbed some weeds under my arm, and that was when I knew I was now veering too far right. I made my way back by keeping my eye on the orange ball ahead. I felt like I had been swimming for hours. I cleared the second orange ball, but I felt as though the swimming would never end. I was tired and coughing up water. I could not see for crap, and my swim cap was full of air and was getting ready to fall off any second, but I could not pull it on or it would slow me down. The cap came off my head about halfway back to shore, and I just let it go. Once the water was shallow enough, I stood up and tried to run, but the water was pulling me down and seemed to weighed a hundred pounds.

I looked behind me for Kat, but I could not see her. I was a little dizzy, and once I reached the sand I had to walk. Why was I so tired? As I entered the open orange fencing, I saw my friends there cheering me on.

"Go, Maddy!"

"You got this!"

"Don't quit," Brad said. "You've trained for this, it's all in your head."

"Run!" Whitney said. "Run!"

I reached my bike and ran it through the parking lot, following the fence. I hopped on and pedaled uphill. My legs were exhausted, but I was glad for the change from swimming. I gave the swim everything I had, but my arms now felt like rubber.

I started to feel the aches in my legs at the five-mile mark. Many women passed me on the road and said, "Good job," or "You're doing great," as they went by. I felt pretty good until a lady who looked to be in her nineties passed me. That was when I pushed everything I had into my legs. I finally reached the orange fencing, but still no sign of Kat.

I started running, but now my legs felt like rubber, too. They no longer knew how to work. I had to walk until my legs figured out the motion of running, and then I took off as fast as I could, but I was struggling to breathe. I saw my friends, but I pretended not to. I was in so much pain I could not even speak. I ran through the grass and followed the path, careful not to lose my balance. Dark spots blurred in my vision, but I would not let myself walk, no way. Brad was right, I trained for this, it was all in my head. I looked back again because I swore I heard my name, but I could not see anyone.

I picked up my pace, but the dark spots took over my vision. And then everything went black.

I OPENED my eyes and stared at an EMT.

"Madeline, can you hear me? My name is Tony and you are in an ambulance on your way to the hospital. Your husband is going to meet us there, okay?"

I nodded my head as much as I could.

"Your friend is here with us."

He leaned forward so I could see the person sitting behind him.

"Kat?" Of all the people in the ambulance with me, I never thought it would be her sitting there.

"Are you okay? I tried to catch you, but you were so fast."

I tried to sit up but dizziness forced me back down. "What happened?"

"You fainted, but you're going to be okay. Brad and everyone else is on their way to the hospital now. They will be right behind us. They couldn't get past the ropes to get in the ambulance so I just hopped in with you. I know we don't know each other that well, but I couldn't let you ride in here alone."

"Hey," the EMT said with a laugh.

"She knows who I am. You may have saved her life, but you're still a complete stranger," she said and smiled to let him know she was joking.

"I'll give you that," he said.

"I'm glad you're both here. Thanks for saving my life."

I AWOKE to hear Brad crying and saying something about how he could not believe it, and Lyndsey was squeezing my hand and squealing with excitement.

"I don't know what you're saying. Please slow down," I said to them.

Brad grabbed my hand in his. "Maddy, you're going to be fine. You were dehydrated, and they gave you an IV, but they ran some tests and well, you're pregnant. We're having a baby."

"Pregnant? Baby?"

The words seemed foreign to me. "How can you be sure?"

"The doctors are sure, we're having a baby."

Was this for real? Was I dreaming? I was not sure how I felt about this. Would this baby be replacing Ariel? How could I have a baby when Ariel would not be a big sister? This made no sense to me. Why were they so happy?

"Isn't that great?"

I stared at him and tried to understand it all. "But what about Ariel? We can't replace Ariel."

He squeezed my hand. "Oh, honey, we aren't replacing Ariel. Nothing or no one could ever replace her." He touched my necklace, and I put my hand over his.

I stared at him until I could process it all. He was right. Nothing would ever replace Ariel. This baby would be Ariel's little sister or brother.

Whitney and Kat came in and congratulated us. They were all smiles and tears.

"I was so scared when you fell," Kat said. "I tried so hard to catch up to you, but you were too fast."

"I'm so glad it wasn't anything serious. You had me so scared," Brad said as he touched his forehead to mine.

I could hardly keep my eyes open.

"Brad," I said, fighting my heavy eyelids.

"Shush," he said. "Just relax. Everything is going to be okay. I'm not going anywhere."

"Promise?"

"I promise. I just have one question for you."

I scrunched up my eyebrows. "What's that?"

"Will you marry me? Again?"

"I thought you'd never ask."